THE
BRIDGE

JESS MOWRY

TO MARK DENNIS

THE
BRIDGE

DOWN!" yelled Bilal, spotting a gun as a minivan skidded around the corner, its ass-end clipping a bag-lady's cart, scattering cans and junk everywhere. The old woman might have seen the steel, but shook her fist and cursed anyway.

The driver almost lost it, but then recovered sloppily and smoked the van to a stop.

Devon had his I-pod cranked, about to go into the liquor store to buy a candy bar, and didn't hear Bilal, who was diving for the ground but tried a desperate tackle.

The AK hammered full-auto, spitting smoke and yellow flame that almost hid the monkey face. Bullets hissed above Bilal as he slammed to dirty concrete. Instinct screamed to hide his head, but he made a grab for Devon's legs. He felt the bullets hitting Devon, tearing into flesh and bone. The liquor store window rippled like a puddle on a windy day, then morphed into a waterfall and spewed between its bars. Something hit the sidewalk amid the crashing glass... Devon's I-pod blown apart. Devon followed seconds later, collapsing half atop Bilal, who sprawled with chest to pavement. Both were shirtless after school, and Devon's blood felt like hot water pouring over Bilal's bare back. The AK went on firing, the monkey face behind it snarling, bullets blasting concrete chips, searching for Bilal.

Bilal snapped awake.

But this wasn't the dream he'd been having for weeks! He heard the same echoes of squealing tires, the same steely stutter of full-auto fire, but it was *his* window exploding! Crystal razors sprayed the room, slashing over his naked body. Bullets sputted into the walls, ripping holes in his movie posters, breaking the backs of his books on the shelves and spewing shreds of paper. The clock on his nightstand tumbled away in a burst of jagged plastic shards, trailing its cord like a wriggling tail. Then his lamp followed, blown apart. A shelf above the bed collapsed, raining books and broken things. Bilal flung himself to the floor and flattened. Would the clip run out before he got hit?

As if in answer to a prayer, the AK fire cut off. But then another took its place as if they were running a relay. Glass in the living room shattered.

"Grandpa! *Jadd!*" Bilal scuttled doglike into the hall as bullets blasted the front of the house, tearing through the interior walls and slashing the air over his head. Chunks of plaster spattered his back as he scrambled along on his hands and knees like a refugee kid being cluster-bombed. "Jadd!" he yelled again. "DOWN!"

Again the gunfire suddenly stopped with the tinny clank of a clip running out. An engine snarled, tires screamed, and a car went screeching up the street as Bilal reached the living room doorway. For a second there was silence, as if the 'hood was holding its breath and wondering who would be next. Then the soundtrack faded back in... a few dogs barking down the block, a siren yelping, coming fast. Bilal's grandfather lay on his mat facing the rosy glow of dawn that turned broken glass into spatters of blood across the Persian carpet.

"Jadd!" Bilal leaped up and ran to the man.

"Be at peace," his grandfather said, turning calmly to face Bilal.

Bilal was panting for breath as if he'd run the middle-school mile. His cheeks were suddenly hot with tears that felt like Devon's blood. He almost puffed a prayer of thanks. "Are you all right?" he asked instead, kneeling beside his grandfather.

"Another war of terror," murmured Jadd Taimur.

Bilal almost spit on the floor. "Monkey-boys with guns!" he snarled, glaring out through fangs of glass where dawn was painting the neighborhood with kinder shades of soft pastels, turning rust to mellow gold and grimy grays to silver. The siren's scream was still approaching, though many blocks away. He looked around the living room at bullet-torn pictures on bullet-pocked walls of bullet-ripped villages in Sudan. A chair and the sofa were bleeding cotton; the TV stared like a jagged skull eye at a shattered vase in a puddle of flowers; and the lamp he'd once thought had belonged to Aladdin was leaking scented oil. "Are you all right?" he asked again.

Bilal's grandfather sat up slowly, a slender man of seventy years with skin of dusky midnight and hair of iron gray. Daggers of glass made musical sounds as they fell from his robe to scatter the floor. "Other than having my prayer interrupted." His onyx eyes ran over Bilal, as naked as his birthing day except for Devon's sliver chain on his chubby chest.

"Are you all right, grandson?"

Bilal became aware of pain; there were cuts on his arms from flying glass, but nothing that would kill him; no wounds like Jadd Taimur had suffered many years ago. No bloody bullet holes like Devon. "Yeah," he said, then added, "I'm sure Allah will understand about your mornin' prayer."

"On whose name be praise."

"...Yeah," said Bilal. "Sure you're okay?"

"I have lived through worse, by Allah's mercy."

"On whose name be praise," said Bilal. It was automatic, like saying wassup when somebody said yo.

A second siren had joined the first, squalling distantly. The barking dogs began to howl. Tires squealed around a corner... an SUV and probably cops. Bilal looked out past shredded drapes that swayed in a salt-scented breeze from the Bay. "I give 'em another minute."

He rose to scan the empty street, where paint-peeling faces of shabby houses stared with blindly curtained eyes. A shade twitched warily here and there, but nobody wanted to witness. ...Or be suspected of witnessing. He tried to smother his panting breaths and listen for sounds of danger -- a car approaching stealthily, coming back to finish the job -- but dogs only howled as the sirens wailed.

3

He spit through a broken window. "Plenty of time for another roll-up, but the monkeys probably don't got the balls."

"We were warned the police would not always be here," said Jadd Taimur, as Bilal helped him rise. More bits of glass rained from his robe to sparkle the floor like junk-shop jewels.

Bilal snorted. "They warned us about a lot of things... *after* they got what they wanted from me!"

"You did what any good man would do."

"...Yeah," said Bilal, and added, "Careful," though his grandfather wore African sandals.

Something sliced the sole of his foot as he picked up his grand-father's walking staff and led him into the kitchen. The window there was still intact, but that probably hadn't been Allah's mercy... the monkeys had *known* when he'd be in his room. And probably when his grandfather prayed.

An SUV in black-and-white smoked to a stop at the curb as Bilal eased his grandfather into a chair at the table already set for Bilal with a bowl and a box of Count Chocula. The ruby and blue of the strobes were dim against the growing day, and the siren cut off, leaving still-howling dogs and the second siren. Heavy boots trampled the porch. Then a fist pounded the door... which was stupid because it was half blown apart. "Oakland police!"

Bilal almost yelled duh, but called instead, "Don't break it down. ...What's left, anyway."

He realized he was naked, but found he didn't give a shit. He stopped in the kitchen doorway, scanning the glittering razors of glass that mined the living room floor. His grandfather offered, "Take my sandals."

"I'm okay," said Bilal, and carelessly went to unlock the door.

The cops were a typical West Oakland team, the older almost as black as Bilal, thirty-something and rolly fat, his belly cascading over his belt and threatening to burst his shirt. The other was blue-eyed and fairly ripped, early-twenties and new to the street, usually letting his partner interpret the baby-talk language of thugs. They had their guns out, and Bilal couldn't hold that against them.

"Jesus!" muttered the white cop as Bilal pulled the splintered door open, sweeping aside a fan of glass. "This looks like Iraq!"

"My grandfather's from Sudan," said Bilal.

"I meant the mess," the cop corrected. "Not the middle-eastern stuff."

"Sudan is in Africa," said Bilal, though not in a smart-ass way.

"Oh." The cop seemed to notice Bilal's nakedness but caught himself before looking surprised.

"You cool, little bro?" asked the black cop, as if naked kids and bullet holes were just a normal part of life.

"Yeah," said Bilal, as the cops crunched in. "My grandfather's okay, too."

"Thank the Good Lord," sighed the black cop. He'd had this watch for a week now ever since the trial; and he'd been the cop who'd saved Bilal, off-duty but packing his Glock -- only a fool wouldn't pack if he could -- on his way to the liquor store to buy a sixer of beer. He'd had more balls than all the monkeys, dropping, and drilling their van a few times, his only cover the bag-lady's cart... after he'd pushed her into a doorway where she had continued to curse.

Real bad men would have reloaded, capped the cop and finished Bilal. ...And probably offed the bag-lady, too. But the monkey-boys had squealed away, their tails between their minivan wheels. Too bad the cop hadn't seen their faces... the bag-lady swore they were Little Grays on a mission of intergalactic terror. Bilal often brought him coffee, the strong, thick brew his grandfather made, and sometimes a box of Safeway donuts while he sat overnight in his car. His name was Akeem but he was a Christian. He wasn't fanatic or boring about it, though he'd given Bilal a Bible last week. But he probably gave everyone Bibles. ...At least anybody he thought could be saved.

"We had to leave," said Akeem, looking a little embarrassed, an expression you seldom saw on a cop. "Sorry, little bro."

The other, named Mark, was looking left-out, like people do when other people are speaking a different language. He added, "Somebody shot up a liquor store over on Adeline Street. We were the closest unit."

"It was probably them," said Akeem, snapping the strap on his holster. "To get us away from your house."

Bilal shrugged. "Monkeys know their jungle."

"Monkeys?" asked Mark. "I thought the gang was called the Dubs."

"They're all stupid monkeys to me!" Bilal glared around at the mess again. "Stupid monkey-boys with guns!"

Akeem frowned. "If you'd come up in this neighborhood you might be a little respectfully scared."

Bilal's eyes narrowed. "Don't gimmie that what it is 'hood shit! I'm scared of dogs with rabies 'cause they're dangerous like Cujo, but I sure as hell don't respect 'em!"

A glass fang dropped from a window frame, and Mark spun around, gripping his gun.

Akeem chuckled. "Chill out, dog."

Bilal's grandfather came in from the kitchen, his sandals softly crunching glass, his staff gently thumping the floor. "Would you gentlemen like coffee?"

Mark hesitated, but Akeem smiled and said, "Thank you, sir."

An ambulance rolled up outside at an almost leisurely pace, its siren trailing off as if bored. Akeem's quick eyes ran over Bilal, noting the cuts on his arms and blood spreading under a foot. "Better let 'em check you out, an' your grandfather, too."

"Not if we gotta pay!" snapped Bilal. He realized again he was naked, but crossed his arms and stood proud.

"I don't know about that, little bro."

"We didn't call it, an' we're not gonna pay for it!"

The EMTs were on the porch, both white, a man and a woman, peering in past the shattered door, their medical boxes in hand. Akeem faced them. "Nobody's hurt. Bill the department."

"You don't have the authority..." the woman EMT began.

"Neither do you," growled Akeem. "So blame it on me an' see where it gets you."

The EMTs traded glances, then shrugged and returned to their idling truck. Akeem spoke into his radio mike, advising someone about something, as Bilal's grandfather reappeared with two small porcelain cups. The rich scent of coffee seemed to banish the stink of hot lead in the air.

"Thank you, sir," said Akeem, accepting a cup and sipping. Mark echoed him, then added surprised, "This is good, Mr. Jadd."

Akeem murmured, "Jadd means grandfather in Arabic. His name is Taimur."

"Oh," said Mark. "It's very good coffee, Mr. Taimur."

Jadd Taimur bowed. "Thank you. And welcome to my home."

What's left anyway, thought Bilal.

He noticed a few of the braver neighbors gathering on the cracked sidewalk beyond the house's little lawn and narrow strip of flower bed. Bilal mowed the lawn on Saturday mornings, pushing an ancient clattering thing that burned his sweat instead of gas, and picked the trash out of the flowers almost every day. He saw an elderly, bathrobed woman, Mrs. Turner, a few houses down, the neighborhood candy lady who also baked supernatural pies... sweet-potato with real whipped-cream. Hers was the only name he knew, though he'd often seen the other faces. A man had a pit-bull on a chain, and Bilal watched it piss on the flowers. There was also a handful of kids with packs on their way to school. Some were pointing at bullet holes and probably guessing the type of gun by the scattered brass in the street.

"Dammit!" muttered Akeem, as two boys snagged souvenirs. "Mark, get those back!"

"Hey!" Mark ran out and the kids ran away.

"Stop!" Mark's hand dropped to his gun, and the kids automatically scattered, becoming multiple targets. Mark could have caught the fattest one or shot a few of the others, but only looked back at Akeem, who sighed.

"String up the tape," called Akeem. "Find out if anyone saw anything. An' don't lose any more evidence." He faced Bilal again. "We'll have to take you to the station. This is a crime scene now""

Bilal glared out at the street. "This whole fuckin' place is a crime scene!" He watched the EMTs roll off. "If you didn't haul the bodies away there'd be more skeletons than people!"

Akeem shrugged. "Get a day off from school."

"I missed two weeks for the goddamn trial. Got a D on my history test."

Akeem's round face looked sad, as did Jadd Taimur's, though Bilal hadn't specified the god. "Pack some things. They'll probably put you up somewhere. In a hotel. At least overnight."

"We're not payin'!" snapped Bilal.

"I'm sure they'll cover it."

"I'm not."

Akeem winced as Bilal crunched away leaving bloody footprints. "Be careful, son!"

"Why?" said Bilal. "I'm already one of the walkin' dead."

TWO

Bilal's grandfather lived simply and clean, just as he'd lived in Sudan. He made a little from painting pictures, mostly of his homeland, but material wealth meant nothing to him. This house was his first with electric lights, running water and telephone; and though it was only a rundown rental he treated it like a museum curator would care for an ancient artifact.

Bilal's room, by contrast, was a sloppy junk shop, though now it looked more like a dump in a war zone. The window glass was totally gone, and the walls of the little Victorian house were nothing but paper to lead. Wooden lathing showed like bones where chunks of plaster were blown away, and most of his classic movie posters -- *Frankenstein, Dracula, Screaming Skull*, and *I Was A Teenage Werewolf* -- hung in shreds like *The Mummy's* rags. Bullets had splintered his DVDs, slain his second-hand TV, killed his clock, slaughtered his lamp, and murdered his little radio. His shelves of books, mostly ghost stories, many bought used from Amazon, might have been good for recycled pulp. His collection of horror magazines, *Fangora, Creepshow*, and *Tales From The Crypt*, lay shredded and scattered like gutter trash. His Dollar Store pack of Milky Way bars was blown in chunks all over floor and looked like the dog shit he scooped off the lawn.

He became aware of pain again, mostly in his bleeding foot. Stepping more carefully now, he went to his bed and looked underneath.... at least his MacBook hadn't been capped. He pulled it out, switched it on and opened a picture file. There was Devon shirtless in jeans, rolly fat and Hershey-bar brown, sprawled upon Bilal's single bed as only a happy fat kid could sprawl, his belly spilling over his thighs, his boy-breasts lolling like melons of Jell-O. In his hands were a Coke and a pizza slice, and on his face his trademark smile. Bilal remembered the D.A.'s questions, the hard wooden chair that stank of lies...

"In your opinion, Bilal, why did they murder your friend?"

"Probably 'cause he smiled at them."

"He was murdered just because he smiled?" The D.A. had turned to the jury, a mix of black, brown and white, some looking shocked, a few not surprised. *"Why would they murder a boy for smiling?"*

Bilal had faced the three monkey-boys, who were dressed in nerdy suits and ties as if they'd been mistakenly busted on their way to Sunday School. They were lean and mean, a health-nazi's dream, strong muscled bodies with sick little minds. He'd made himself smile in their hating faces. *"If you smile at a monkey it pisses him off. He thinks you ain't afraid of him. Or worse you might be laughin' at him for bein' a stupid monkey."*

If looks could have killed he would have been dust, like a vampire toasted under the sun.

The defense attorney objected, and the judge had sustained it, giving the monkeys all the rights Devon never had.

Bilal smiled now at Devon's picture. Anyone would... except a monkey. Devon had been his only friend since he'd come to West Oakland, though it felt like they'd been homies for life. Devon was an enigma, something that couldn't be explained. He was "out of shape" and didn't want in, refusing to run the middle-school mile and cheerfully taking an F in P.E. Bilal had walked the laps beside him, also defiantly getting an F despite the coach's warning that it would go on his PERMANENT RECORD. Devon's grades had only been average, but all the dudes he'd helped with homework -- including Bilal -- had aced their tests. Devon never fought anyone but nobody tested or bullied him. He didn't smoke weed or do any drugs, and his only sin had been smiling at stupid monkey-boys.

"Why?" Bilal asked the picture.

Devon should have known better... he *had* known better! Even Bilal from the middle-class 'burbs had learned in a week to drop his eyes and keep his face an empty mask when monkeys flexed at him.

He gazed at Devon's picture... Devon's digital remains. It must have been the warm afternoon, the peaceful park where they'd lost their shirts, the leaf-dappled sun playing over their chests as they'd lain in the grass beneath a tree. And the forty-ounce they were sharing; that friendly buzz you got from brew that made you want to hug everyone. Like, who could hate on a day like that when Allah seemed to be blessing the world? The monkeys had wanted their tree. ...If only Devon had at least acted scared!

Bilal shut down and closed the computer, then scanned the ravaged remains of his room. The bullets had missed the closet door mirror, and the glass showed a dusky-black boy of thirteen. He was probably built to be muscular, and might have been if he'd wanted to, but his biceps were roundly padded with chub and his chest was a pair of ebony orbs that jiggled and bobbed when he moved, while his belly was like a slab of soft blubber swagging almost over his shaft, its navel a cave into midnight. His face was still childlike with cherubic cheeks, a wide snubby nose and full pouty lips; and his hair was a mop of shoulder-length dreads -- because that had been Devon's style – shadowing onyx anime eyes. Devon's chain gleamed around his neck, its silver pendant, the head of Anubis, the Egyptian jackal god of the dead, nestled between the spheres of his chest. It had no special significance except Devon had liked it, and Bilal had bought it for him last year in a shabby pawnshop. It might have been buried with Devon, but his mom had wanted Bilal to have it.

Bilal glanced again at his bed. The early October night had been warm -- some people called it Indian Summer – and he'd slept with the blanket down to his waist so the sheet was covered with glittering glass, chunks of plaster and shreds of books. He tore off the bedding and flung it away, then sat on the mattress to check his foot. The gash wasn't deep, though still oozing blood. His other wounds were baby-ass. On his desk was a bottle of alcohol for cleaning his DVDs, and somehow it had survived. He poured a little on his foot and muttered a curse at the sting. A plain white T-shirt lay on the floor along with yesterday's jeans and socks. He snagged the shirt, shook off the glass, and wiped the blood from his other cuts.

"Bilal?" called Akeem from the living room. "Best hurry up, the suits are comin'. They'll axe you all the same questions they gonna axe at the station. No point in answerin' everything twice."

Bilal snarled back, "They'll axe 'em a million times anyway an' still won't believe the answers!"

"Want me to have a look at your foot?"

"No! ...But thanks."

He got up and opened a dresser drawer, which fell apart in his hands. He checked the boxers inside for holes and found a pair with only one. Then he snagged his jeans, shook off the glass, and pulled them up to casual sag beneath his bobbly belly. Like the shorts, the jeans had been Devon's, and both were way too big. Devon's belt with steel studs was the only thing that kept them on. Bilal snagged fresh socks, tied his sneaks, then scanned the ruined room again. What else should he take? It suddenly seemed like everything mattered, all he'd collected in thirteen years. He remembered one of his grandfather's proverbs: *In the course of a long life, a wise man is prepared to abandon his baggage more than once.*

Akeem was the only cop he trusted, but they wouldn't leave him to guard the house. And yellow tape was no defense, no pentagram or evergreen, no crescent, cross, or Voodoo charm, against the creatures of the night who roamed this soulless neighborhood.

He picked up his pack from the floor: who gave a shit about home-work when monkeys were trying to kill you? He dumped the books and binder out, stuffed in shorts, a pair of socks, then his precious laptop. What else was really important? His autographed glossy of Freddie Kruger? No, that was little-kid shit, like a six-year-old packing to run away. A lot of his life was in the computer. He could always read books on the web, finish the H. P. Lovecraft story, *The Shadow Over Innsmouth* -- the book had been brutally blasted -- watch a movie, hear a tune. And Devon lived in there.

His eye fell on the nightstand. His Quran lay there as always, though he hadn't read it in almost a year. He stuck it in the drawer each night, but every day when he got home there it was again.

Beside the Quran was the Bible Akeem had given to him. Both had somehow survived the attack, though probably by random luck and not some holy force-field. Bilal had read the Bible and had felt defiant doing so. But his grandfather hadn't said anything, and the Quran was simply there each night beside the other book.

Bilal didn't see much difference. Both books said to love everyone, then made a one-eighty and told you to hate. Both pleaded for peace, then justified war. Both promised rewards if you were good, but only after you were dead.

Maybe Devon knew the truth.

Bilal put the books in the drawer. Let them fight it out. And, who in this 'hood would want either one?

He put on another white T-shirt – also Devon's, baggy and big, draping him midway to his knees -- then snagged a brown leather bomber jacket. The jacket had also been Devon's but he'd gotten too fat to zip it this summer; a summer spent mostly here in this room, playing games, watching TV, surfing the web and stuffing down snacks... Devon's mom worked at Grocery Outlet and got a discount on Twinkies, cupcakes, donuts and pies. They'd both packed on about thirty pounds safe from the street in their sanctuary, though it had hardly shown on Devon. He'd stayed overnight, often for days, his rolly weight overloading the bed and making it creak like an old skeleton, usually sweaty but not smelling bad. They'd made up stories there in the dark, scaring each other with werewolves and wraiths, vampires, zombies, and graveyard ghouls, while gunshots popped in the alleys and streets and sirens screamed like banshees. His mom had given his things to Bilal after Devon's funeral, along with the Anubis charm. Bilal pressed the jacket to his face, hiding his tears in soft sheepskin where Devon's scent still lingered like a faint and friendly ghost.

THREE

"I heard Buckwheat became a Muslim… changed his name to *Kareem* Of Wheat."

Both cops laughed, a black and a white, down by the vending machines. Bilal shot a glare at their bulletproof backs, then glanced at Jadd Taimur beside him, who was clad in a kufi and African robe. But, maybe the cops hadn't seen him and were only sharing an asshole joke? And maybe his grandfather hadn't heard; he was a little hard of hearing from a bomb blast in Sudan.

They were sitting on a hard plastic bench out in a hall that reeked of cops… leather, steel and gun oil, deodorants and aftershave, and acid pepper spray. The place was a kind of go-to-hell clean, cleaned by people paid to clean who really didn't give a shit, but the walls were slimed with fear and lies like evil ectoplasm. The overhead lights were painfully bright as if designed to kill disease, and the bench seemed to hate being sat on like a pissy cat ready to bite.

Jadd Taimur's VISITOR pass was clipped to his robe, while Bilal's was snapped to the tail of his shirt and dangled between his out-spread legs. A few passing cops said "excuse me" and Bilal would pull back his feet, but most looked like they wanted to kick him and only glowered when going around. They had taken his grandfather's staff again as soon as he'd walked in the door, almost snatching it away as if it was a wizard's weapon.

Akeem had heard the other cop's joke, scowling now as he came up the hall. He offered Bilal a McDonalds bag. "Brought y'all break-fast sandwiches."

Bilal's belly growled at the rich scents of sausage and hot melted cheese. "My grandfather doesn't eat pork."

"Oh. Sorry, Mr. Taimur," said Akeem.

Jadd Taimur smiled. "All deeds are made complete by their intentions. I am sure my grandson can eat two."

Bilal hesitated before opening the bag, but his grandfather added, "You need your strength."

Akeem indicated the vending machines. "Can I get you some coffee, Mr. Taimur?"

"Thank you but I am fine."

Akeem smiled. "I wouldn't drink that slop, either. ...I gotta leave, but I'll try an' check on your house later on." He glanced at a door beside the bench, where a plastic sign read

LT. DOBBIN
HOMICIDE

"Hope he don't keep you waitin' too long."

"We're used to it," said Bilal, sinking his teeth in a juicy sandwich.

Akeem gave Bilal a pat on the shoulder. "'Even youths grow tired and weary, an' young men stumble an' fall; but those who hope in the Lord will always renew their strength.'"

Bilal replied, "'Allah creates you weak. After weakness He gives you strength.'"

"On whose name be praise," said Jadd Taimur. "Thank you for all you have done, Akeem."

Anger flickered across Akeem's face. "We really ain't done jack."

"You saved my life," said Bilal.

"Wish I coulda got there sooner."

Bilal touched Devon's charm on his chest. "So do I."

"I'll check back," said Akeem, then walked away down the hall and shoved between the two other cops, making one spill his coffee so it looked like he'd wet himself.

The detective's door opened and a woman came out. She was sobbing, her eyes streaming tears. She looked like one of the monkey boys' moms when her son had been sentenced to twenty-five years -- a mother could still love a stupid monkey -- but no, Bilal saw, she wasn't.

Maybe her son had been monkey-boy prey?

Detective Dobbin scowled from the doorway as if expecting a garbage truck making deliveries. He was forty-something with graying brown hair and weary blue eyes; and except for a Glock in a shoulder holster, looked like a middle-school football coach whose team never won any games. "Come in," he said, though his tone was more like *not today* when Jehovahs came.

Bilal had finished the first sandwich. He put the second, partly-chomped, back in the still-warm bag, then helped his grandfather to his feet and offered a shoulder to lean on.

Dobbin's office never changed, cluttered with papers and stacks of folders, reeking of fear-sweat and slimy with lies. The dented waste-basket still overflowed with fast-food wrappers and crushed coffee cups. The computer screen still looked like a sneeze. One tube in the overhead light still flickered just enough to annoy. Amid the mur-derous mess on the desk was a framed picture of two fat boys, maybe ten and twelve. Both were stuffed in swimming trunks and holding fishing poles in a boat. They looked like they were having fun. There was also a plastic trophy with WORLD'S GREATEST DAD on its base.

Dobbin plopped behind the desk and snatched a paper coffee cup as Bilal eased his grandfather into a chair... maybe the one the woman had cried on. Bilal took another chair beside it, slumping down like a bored little kid and pulling the sandwich out of the bag.

"I'm sorry about what happened this morning," said Dobbin, like an undertaker saying, "so sorry for your loss."

"Yeah," said Bilal, his mouth full again.

"We're investigating."

"Yeah," said Bilal, and half muffled a burp.

"Did you see their faces?"

"No," said Bilal.

Dobbin gave him a cop look. "If you had would you tell me?"

Bilal shrugged. "I don't know anymore."

Jadd Taimur said, "I am sure he would."

Dobbin looked a light-year from sure, but opened a folder and skimmed a form. "None of your neighbors saw anything, but we're sure it was the Dubs."

Bilal ate the last bite of sandwich. "Duh," he muttered, then blasted a burp that scented the air with meat and cheese.

Dobbin glared. "What did you expect?"

"Exactly what we got," said Bilal, slumping even more in the chair in a defiantly bratty kid way and splaying out his legs, his sneaker soles displayed to Dobbin, who of course didn't understand.

Jadd Taimur said quietly, "Bilal did what any good man would do."

"Yeah, I know," said Dobbin, and some of the anger left his face. "You seem like decent people, but the system isn't set up to protect... After the fact, I mean."

"Not people like us, you mean," said Bilal.

Dobbin frowned. "There isn't a witness protection program. Not for a *case* like this. The accused has a right to face their accuser."

"But I don't have any right to live?"

Dobbin gulped coffee like medicine that tasted as bad as it smelled. "What I'm trying to say..."

Bilal scowled and sat up straight. "Monkeys killed a black kid, an' nobody gives a shit if they kill another one."

Dobbin looked pissed for a moment, but shrugged. "I don't make the laws." He again raised his cup but found it empty, crushed it like he was killing something and dropped it into the brimming wastebasket, where it rolled off and fell on the floor. "There's a victims assistance agency, but I don't know how much help they can be."

"So, we're back to bein' victims again."

Dobbin's phone rang and he grabbed it like a squalling cat he wanted to strangle. "Yeah? ...Give me five minutes." Then he turned to Jadd Taimur. "If I were you I'd move. ...Fast. I can give you another week of protection..." He shot a warning look at Bilal. "That should be enough to make your arrangements, and Victims Assistance might help with that. I'll give you their card. They also have a website..."

Bilal snorted again. "I got a computer, believe it or not."

"The Dubs are only a small local gang..." Dobbin went on to Jadd

Taimur as if Bilal was already a ghost just making annoying noises. "...mostly dealing crack to kids, and don't have any connections. I doubt they could track anyone very far. That would take brains." He picked up another folder and flipped through some papers inside. "Not one of those punks finished high-school, and two dropped out of eighth grade. ...Does Bilal have any relatives? Hopefully in another town?"

Bilal spoke first, "When my parents got killed in a car crash I went to live with Jadd Taimur."

"We could put you in a foster home."

"No! An' that wouldn't help my grandfather. If they can't kill me they'll go after him."

Dobbin sighed. "I know. But it would be less conspicuous if he resettled alone. ...On the down-low."

"Less conspicuous," said Bilal, precisely pronouncing the word.

"...Then, maybe after a few months..."

Bilal snarled, "I ain't gettin' stuck in no fuckin' home!"

"Don't fight me, kid!" roared Dobbin. "I don't have to do a god-damn thing!"

Then his eyes went to the picture of the two fat boys in the boat. "Look, I'm sorry your friend was killed. ...And I'm sorry about all the other shit. *Nobody* should have to go through that. But some people do and they come out okay. If you let it screw up the rest of your life, the... monkeys... killed you anyway."

Jadd Taimur spoke, "Bilal has a cousin."

"...What?" cried Bilal.

"Actually, you have two, and the younger would be about your age."

For a second Bilal sat stunned. Then he asked, "Doesn't that mean I have an uncle?"

"He passed away some years ago," Jadd Taimur replied. "But your elder cousin would be in his twenties, and from what I know of them, your younger cousin lives with him."

Dobbin cocked his head. "Where?"

"They live near a town called Stockton, in what I believe is called the Delta."

"That should be far enough," said Dobbin. "Mostly farm country up there. A few of... your people... but probably not muzzlem." He glanced at Bilal. "But he doesn't look muzzlem without the hat."

Bilal had turned to his grandfather. "How come I didn't know I had cousins? Why didn't mom an' dad tell me? ...Or you?"

"I will explain later," said Jadd Taimur.

"So?" asked Dobbin, checking his watch. "You think he could live with his cousins until you get resettled?"

"I will write to them," said Jadd Taimur.

The telephone squalled and Dobbin snatched it. "...Okay, send 'em in." He tossed the two folders aside, snagged another from a pile, then turned to Jadd Taimur again. "I hope you get a quick answer."

FOUR

"They're out there," said Bilal, scanning the almost empty street as dawn light painted the neighborhood with gentle shades of rose and gold.

"You see anything last night?" asked Mark.

"I can smell their monkey shit."

Akeem was also scoping the street as they stood on the house's front porch. The black-and-white was at the curb, exhaust pipe trailing a ghost of steam in the morning coolness. "Probably 'round the corner up there. They tried to follow the movin' van yesterday afternoon."

"They did?" asked Bilal, who wore only jeans slipping low on his hips, their tumbled cuffs concealing bare feet and his belly lolling over in front.

"Yeah," said Mark. "We gave them a ticket."

"For what?" asked Bilal, eating the last of a Pop-Tart.

"Running a stop sign." Mark scowled. "If this was Iraq..."

"But it ain't," said Akeem. "So don't go gettin' no wack ideas."

"Goddammit!" snapped Mark. "We know they want to kill Bilal. We know they tried to kill him. And we know they're *going* to kill him if they get a chance! And all we can do is give them a ticket!"

"What did you do in Iraq?" asked Bilal.

"Killed people who were trying to kill me."

"'Think not that I bring you peace,'" said Bilal. "'I bring a sword.'"

"Is that in the Quran?" asked Mark.

"No. The Bible. Jesus said it."

"Sounds like He was in Iraq."

20

"This ain't Iraq," Akeem said again.

"I noticed," said Mark. "Here we just give the terrorists tickets."

The living room windows had been covered with plywood, and the house was neat and clean again thanks to Jadd Taimur... except for all the bullet holes. Bilal had mowed the lawn yesterday because his grandfather had asked him to, and picked the trash out of the flowers, though that didn't make any sense... the landlord had threatened to sue for the damage, but Akeem had had a word with him. Probably more than one.

Mark looked in though the open front door, now held together with new yellow boards that smelled like Devon's Christmas trees. "How many times does your grandfather pray?"

"Five times a day," said Bilal. "At least."

"Facing the sun?"

"Facin' Mecca."

"How does he know exactly?" asked Mark. "I mean, the earth is round."

"The Quran says, 'All deeds are made complete by their intentions.' Like, Allah knows when you're doin' your best even if you don't get it right."

"Don't you pray?" asked Akeem.

"Last time I prayed was on the sidewalk when... I prayed that Devon would live." Bilal glanced in at his grandfather and lowered his voice. "But maybe Allah didn't care 'cause he wasn't one of the Faithful."

He almost added that maybe Jesus hadn't cared either because Devon hadn't been a Christian, but didn't want to hurt Akeem's feelings.

Akeem's face saddened anyway. "You an' Devon was pretty tight."

Bilal touched Devon's necklace. "Yeah. ...When do you pray?"

"Every night," said Akeem. "Been prayin' for you an' your grandfather."

"...Thanks," said Bilal. "He's been prayin' for you an' Mark."

"Thanks," said Mark. "I could probably use it."

Bilal shrugged. "Thank him. But thanks for takin' our backs... both of you. An' don't shit me 'it's just your job.'"

Akeem sighed. "I used to think it was." He glanced at his watch. "Better get dressed, little bro… all the way. The car should be here for your grandfather soon."

The house was as empty inside as a skull, and Bilal's bare feet made ghostly echoes that followed him into his room. He paused for a second to listen -- Devon had always gone barefoot here -- but the padding of feet had stopped when he had. His window had also been boarded and his room was spooky and dark. He'd saved everything worth saving, packed it all in a crate yesterday, and spent last night on the floor in a blanket with Devon's jacket for a pillow. He picked up the jacket and slipped it on, the sheepskin soft against his skin, the scent of Devon haunting his nose.

The power had been cut off -- a city inspector had called it unsafe – but Bilal had patched "Aladdin's lamp," using a cork from an old wine bottle and read by its gentle flame at night, comparing the Bible to the Quran and finding no comfort in either. His pack was packed with a few extra clothes, toothbrush, paste, shorts and socks. He'd also packed the holy books, though he wasn't sure why, and a last white T-shirt hung like a ghost from a nail where Freddie Kruger had been. Bilal sat on the floor to tie his sneaks, then removed Devon's jacket to put on the shirt.

"Bilal? Car's here," called Akeem. "You dressed... all the way?"

"Yeah." Bilal put on the jacket again, zipped it up though the morning was warm, and slung his pack over a shoulder. He paused in the bullet-ripped doorway, feeling an urge to whisper goodbye. ...Goodbye to what, he wondered? This shabby old house in this sick neighborhood? If Devon's ghost was still around he wanted it to follow him.

The car was unmarked and rat-colored gray, though any street kid would have known what it was. An unmarked cop was waiting beside it. Jadd Taimur was out on the porch in kufi and robe, his mat rolled neatly under an arm. He embraced Bilal. "I hope it will not be long until we are together again."

"I hope so, too," said Bilal, hugging his grandfather tightly.

"You have your cousins' address?"

Bilal patted a pocket. "Yeah."

"Goodbye, then, for now, grandson."

"Goodbye, Jadd."

"Remember, you did the right thing."

"Yeah," said Bilal. "...May Allah be with you."

"On whose name be praise. And He is always with you, Bilal."

Akeem and Mark stood flanking Bilal, watching the street as the car rolled away. Window shades twitched in several houses, but no one had come out to witness. Even the kids in the neighborhood had been taking a long way to school.

"How you feelin'?" asked Akeem.

Bilal was gazing after the car. "Wish I knew where he was goin'."

"Dobbin thought it best you didn't."

"'Cause I might try an' go there?"

"What do you think?"

"That he thinks I'm stupid."

"Think the Dubs are watching?" asked Mark as the car disappeared around a corner.

"Yeah," said Bilal and Akeem together. Akeem added, "But they probably won't follow it. There's only five of 'em left, an' one ain't old enough to drive."

"Won't they recruit new members?" asked Mark.

"Sure," said Akeem. "But, hard as it might be to believe, a lot of kids are gettin' a clue that thugger shit is..."

Bilal spit on the newly-mown lawn. "Nothin' but stupid monkeys playin' bang-bang you dead on the real."

Akeem checked the quiet street again. A seagull cried from a telephone pole where sneaker-fruit hung from a wire. A sleepy dog barked a few houses down; a rat scuttled into a gutter drain; and a garbage truck rumbled a block away. "This is the best time to hit us. Flex their power here in the 'hood. I asked Dobbin for backup but he said he couldn't spare it."

"Couldn't, or wouldn't?" said Bilal.

"Don't go paranoid on me. You gettin' capped won't help his career, an' he's already done a lot more than he had to." Akeem scanned around again. "Hopefully they think we got backup 'cause this would be the place to have it."

Mark muttered, "Wish I had my M-16."

"Don't go getting' no PTS; you fightin' American terror now."

Mark unsnapped his pistol. "Like fighting a tank with a BB gun."

"That's the way I always been fightin'."

Mark shook his head. "I killed a kid about Bilal's age. He had a bomb strapped to his chest, trying to take out a tank."

Akeem shrugged. "I killed a pretty young woman comin' at me with a butcher knife. She'd just cut her two-year-old's throat... 'cause her boyfriend didn't like him cryin'. If you need an enemy who believes in somethin', best get back in the Army."

He and Mark still flanking Bilal, they came down the sidewalk across the lawn and past the strip of flowerbed where a new crop of trash was already sprouting. "Squeeze up front with us," said Akeem as Mark cracked the passenger door.

"Yeah," added Mark. "We're bullet-resistant."

"Don't you mean bullet-proof?" asked Bilal, touching Mark's Kevlar vest.

"Depends on the size of the bullets."

"Wait," said Bilal, and went to the mailbox.

Akeem and Mark tensed as a car started up on the next block. "C'mon, Bilal!" ordered Akeem.

Bilal had already opened the box. "Got my new *Creepshow.*"

"Move it!" yelled Mark as the car came toward them. He boosted Bilal in the black-and-white, then dropped to a crouch behind the door.

Akeem, on the driver's side in the street, relaxed as the car murmured past. "Just somebody goin' to work. Folks around here still do that. ...The lucky ones got jobs, anyway."

"Didn't you stop your mail?" asked Mark, as they rolled up the street in the morning sunlight.

Sandwiched tightly between the two men, breathing their scents of gun oil and leather, Bilal looked up from his magazine. "I was waitin' for this. Dobbin said don't leave a forward address 'cause it might be tracked on the Internet... if the monkeys could use a computer."

Akeem frowned a little, checking the mirrors as he turned a

corner. "He ain't no expert at this kinda thing. His job is fillin' up privatized prisons. ...What about your family an' friends? The Dubs could get their addresses by goin' through your mailbox."

"Don't got no friends," said Bilal, "since Devon..." He sighed. "No family neither except my cousins, an' I just found out about them. We only get bills an' junk mail. Plus my magazines; an' I'll start a new subscription after I get to my cousins'."

Akeem punched through a yellow light, keeping his eyes on the mirror. "Wish we had time to roll through McDees."

"Me too," said Bilal.

"Might as well finish these donuts." Akeem gave Bilal a Dunkin' box with six creme-filled remaining.

Mark had been watching the right-hand mirror. "How come you just found out you had cousins?"

Bilal replied with his mouth full, "My dad had an older brother, but nobody ever told me. Guess he was kinda bad or somethin'. Dropped out of school an' disappeared."

"Black sheep of the family?" asked Mark. "...Sorry."

Bilal laughed. "Guess he was. But, he wrote to Jadd a few years ago. I think he wanted to find my dad an' maybe try an' get back together. But then he got killed in an accident... somethin' about a bridge. His oldest son... one of my cousins... only wrote once after that. My younger cousin's about my age... he's the one who answered Jadd, sayin' I could stay with them."

Akeem smiled. "That should be cool for both of you. Lots of our folk in Stockton, but we spread pretty thin in the Delta."

Mark asked, "What about your cousins' mother? You never mentioned an aunt."

Bilal messily ate another donut. "My uncle never said nothin' about her when he wrote to Jadd."

"Do your cousins know why you're coming?"

"Dobbin said not to tell 'em... just say my grandfather had to move an' I needed a place to stay awhile."

"You gonna tell 'em?" asked Akeem.

Bilal licked creme off his fingers. "Dobbin said to be careful about tellin' people what happened to me. But, I think they got a right to know."

"We got monkeys," muttered Mark, gazing into the mirror.

"Hey, hey," said Akeem. "…Little joke."

"Very little," said Mark. "All five of 'em in a minivan. Looks like mom's taxi with babies on board."

"I noticed," said Akeem. "Probably boosted, run the plate."

Mark tapped keys on the dashboard computer. "Why some nerdy minivan? I thought thugs rolled bad-ass rides."

"Low-pro on a mission," said Akeem. "Nobody remembers a mini-van, except it was a minivan, an' there's plenty of room for the posse. Nice big windows to shoot from, an' usually easy to steal. 'Specially up in white neighborhoods. Daddy's Hot Wheels gets the Lo-Jack. But Mommy's ride has the Playskool alarm an' spends the night in the driveway 'cause the two-car garage is half full of toys, like campin' gear an' fitness machines." He put a hand on Bilal's shoulder. "Don't turn around. We don't wanna scare the monkeys away."

FIVE

Still got our monkey tail?" asked Akeem, as they neared the railroad station.

A train was slowly approaching, rumbling south past Jack London Square where tracks ran down the middle of the street, cars darting aside like mice from a cat.

"Yeah," said Mark, as Akeem stopped in a red zone about thirty feet from the station doors. "They cut in behind that roach coach."

The sidewalk bustled with mostly white people, many lugging or pulling suitcases; families with kids, the kids with packs, hurrying into the station. The building was fronted with glass, and Bilal could see it was crowded inside.

Akeem shut off the engine. "This is the next best place for a hit. Blow up in the papers an' get on TV. Send a message the Dubs are 'bad,' an' make little monkeys wanna be big ones."

Mark nodded. "Join a gang and be all you can be."

"Usually twenty-five to life... or forever in a grave." Akeem scanned the busy station. "We know they got at least two AKs. Could make a hell of a mess in there. No hoo-rah shit if it happens, Mark. Cover an' call for backup."

"Understood," said Mark.

Akeem faced Bilal. "You down with the plan?"

Bilal swallowed a last bite of donut and licked his fingers again. "Let's do this."

Akeem checked his watch as the train rumbled in, brake shoes squealing as it stopped, massive engine shaking the ground as it came to a low-thunder idle. Porters, all black, began opening doors, and people got off toting luggage.

"Wait five minutes," Akeem said to Mark. "The monkeys are out of their jungle here so they gonna be scared an' confused. One's gotta wait in the car... probably one with a license, so two don't have much experience. They might freeze up, or freak an' run. Or they might spray anything that moves. ...Don't shoot first."

He studied the building again. "If any of 'em got a spoonful of brains they know there's cameras all over this place so they probably gonna hood-up. If security here is worth a shit they'll probably spot 'em an' come on the run. That might scare 'em off... or make 'em start shootin'." He glanced at the outside mirror. "The two younger ones are across the street. Baggy an' saggy. Got bananas... I mean band-anas."

"I see 'em," said Mark, checking his mirror. "Probably keeping in touch by phone... yeah, little baggy just made a call."

"If I was the other two," said Akeem, "I'd come around that shuttle bus an' hit you before you get inside."

"Understood," said Mark.

Akeem gave Bilal a pat on the shoulder. "Trust in the Lord, little bro."

"Right now I trust in you," said Bilal.

Akeem popped his door. "Five minutes, then go."

"Don't worry," said Mark to Bilal, as Akeem got out and walked away, heading for the idling train where people were starting to board. "I never lost a man in my squad." He watched as Akeem spoke to a porter and climbed aboard one of the cars. Then he pulled something out of a pocket. "You know how to use one of these?"

Bilal regarded the gun. It looked like an old Army .45, squarish in shape, dented and scarred. One of the black plastic grips was crack-ed, and most of the blue was worn off the steel. "I never *shot* a gun."

"If a monkey can shoot, so can you. ...Maybe that didn't come out right."

"That's cool, I know what you mean."

"This is a Tokarev, Model TT. 7.62. Ugly, but built like a Mack garbage truck. Used to be Soviet Army, see the Red star on the grips?"

"Yeah."

"Eight shot clip, you cock it like this. No manual safety, understand?"

"...Yeah."

"Only safe way to pack it is without a round in the chamber... nothing in the hole."

"...Okay."

"There's one in it now," said Mark. "Pull the trigger, it will shoot. And seven more times if you need to."

"...Aight," said Bilal, taking the gun.

"It's clean," added Mark. "At least in this country. I brought it home for a souvenir."

"From somebody else you killed in the war?"

"At least he believed in something." Mark checked his watch. "Keep it until you don't need it. Until you're sure you don't need it. Then throw it away where nobody can find it. There's a lot of rivers where you're going."

"...Okay." Bilal slipped the gun in his jacket pocket.

"Remember, there's no safety," said Mark. "Unload it as soon as you can... pull the clip and cock it again to pop out the round in the chamber. Keep your finger off the trigger while you're doing that. Understood?"

"Yeah."

"Akeem doesn't know about this."

"I figured that," said Bilal. "You could get in trouble, huh?"

Mark laughed. "I just gave a gun to a Muslim kid; they'd probably waterboard me at Gitmo." He checked his watch again. "It's showtime. Stay ahead of me through the doors. Once we're inside be ready to run."

"Understood," said Bilal, tugging his pack straps tighter. "An' thanks."

Mark shrugged. "I gotta believe in something, and it might as well be you."

Bilal squirmed past the steering wheel, bulky in his jacket and pack. Mark came around and opened the door, flicking his eyes across the street, then to the idling bus. Bilal slid out, catching a glimpse of one of the Dubs, maybe fifteen, his face in shadow under his hood, bandana hiding all but his eyes. Then he spotted two bigger boys edging around the bus.

"Go!" ordered Mark, shoving Bilal through the station doorway.

A group of people were just coming out, burdened by luggage and totes. Mark used Bilal as a battering ram, like women used babies in strollers at malls, his uniform muting the people's curses. A man's voice announced through speakers: *"Coast Starlight now departing for San Jose, Salinas, Paso Robles, San Luis Obispo, Santa Barbara, Oxnard, Simi Valley, Van Nuys, and Los Angeles. ...All aboard!"*

The place was a jumble of images, like someone had dropped a video cam... polished floor, rows of chairs, people hugging and saying goodbyes. Bilal saw a white kid staring at him because he was being pushed by a cop. A woman glared at Mark when he bumped her. A security guard had noticed them and was starting across the room.

Bilal looked over his shoulder: three of the Dubs, two big, one small, were trying to get through the doors, but people weren't getting out of their way. A man in a suit shoved the younger Dub back.... no respect for monkeys here. That meant their steel was still on the under.

"I see 'em," said Mark, still bulling Bilal toward the platform doors, people looking pissed at first but then backing off because he was a cop.

"But, there's only three," puffed Bilal, getting his breath battered out against bodies.

"I noticed, keep going!"

Outside, porters were closing doors as the last of the passengers boarded the train. Hands were waving behind window glass. The big diesel rumbled, powering up. Most of the people inside the station were moving toward the street doors. Angry murmurs and curses were growing as the Dubs shoved their way against the flow like wankster salmon fighting upstream.

"Don't look!" said Mark. "They're my problem now."

They had almost reached the platform doors, now being closed by another guard. The first guard, white and somewhere in his forties, a small .38 in his holster, had wormed his way through the people.

"What's going on?" he demanded.

Mark didn't stop. "Those three black kids in hoodies back there. ...Don't look at them! See any action?"

"...Yeah, in the Gulf."

"Then you don't wanna see any more in here."

"What should I do?"

"Nothing unless they start shooting, and call 911 if they do. Don't try for a medal, they got us outgunned, and we don't want collateral damage."

"Understood!"

The crowd, like a big sleepy animal, was slowly becoming aware that something was burrowing into its fur. Curses were getting louder as the Dubs pushed people out their way. Somebody yelled, "Security!"

"Open that door!" ordered Mark, as the other guard moved to close it.

The train's whistle blew. Compressed air hissed as brakes released. Suddenly there were screams of terror.

"They pulled!" puffed Bilal as he burst into sunlight.

"Surprised they waited this long," muttered Mark. "...NO!" he yelled to the second guard, whose hand was going for his gun. "They'll blow you apart! Cover!"

More screams echoed inside the station as if the living dead were loose. The crowd had parted like the Red Sea, a few people diving onto the floor, some pulling children with them, as the three hooded boys, two with AKs, the smaller with some kind of pistol, awkward in their ass-baring jeans, came charging for the doors.

Smoke pillared up from the engine; the train was beginning to move.

"There!" yelled Mark, stabbing a finger three cars down where a porter leaned out of a still-open door. "Go! Go! Go!"

Bilal dashed for the door as the car drew closer. He hadn't run for maybe two years, and his chest and belly wobbled and bobbed beneath the bulky jacket; and even though he wore Devon's belt his jeans were slipping down.

"GO!" Mark shouted again.

Bilal blew a second glancing back, seeing Mark with his gun in both hands drop to a soldier's crouch on the platform.

The monkeys burst out of the station, skidding cartoonishly to a stop and slamming into each other like a Three Stooges movie. Mark could have shot them all right then and solved a lot of problems for a lot of people.

The car with the open door was nearing. The porter scoped the scene and jerked his head inside. Bilal expected gunfire, but heard Mark yell, "Don't try it!"

The car was rolling past Bilal, its open door just six feet away, when he caught a glimpse of a fourth hooded boy who'd come around outside the building, armed with maybe a Cobray. Bilal remembered an old war movie. "Mark! Three o'clock!"

The train was gathering speed. Bulked by his jacket and pack, Bilal made a clumsy dive for the door. He grabbed a metal handle but his sneakers slipped off the step, kicking air above the tracks. But a hand reached out and gripped his arm, pulling him inside. There was a short burst of fire... Cobrays were famous for jamming. Bullets rattled on steel. Something hit his back like a fist, knocking him forward onto the floor.

"Lord!" cried the porter, dragging Bilal clear of the steps then slamming the door behind him. Bilal heard a shot from a pistol... Mark's. He expected full-auto rips in return, but only heard the diesel drone and the clatter and creak of the car.

"Son!" cried the porter, and dropped to his knees beside Bilal.

"I'm... okay," panted Bilal, almost surprised he was.

"Thank god!" The man hauled Bilal to his feet as if he was somebody's luggage. "Thought I was back in 'Nam for minute. ...Hurry up now."

The door across the car was still open. Rolling past were gravel and weeds; beyond was a chain-link fence. Bilal faced the front of the train and jumped, hitting the ground at a clumsy run and almost losing his jeans beneath the plunge of his belly blubber. He stumbled away from the click-clacking wheels and jammed his back to the fence.

"Glad I could help!" called the porter, leaning from the doorway. "Whatever that was all about!"

Bilal waved to the man while panting for breath as the last of the cars went rumbling by in a swirl of dust and a flutter of trash. Inside a window four feet away a boy with a laptop was playing a game. The train's whistle blew at a crossing, where red lights flashed and warning bells clanged. Bilal was about two blocks from the station. He didn't hear any more gunfire, but several sirens screamed.

Then, a white Ford Explorer came rolling up through dry yellow weeds on the other side of the fence, the sun gleaming bright on its twenty-inch rims. "You okay, little bro?" asked Akeem at the wheel.

"Yeah," puffed Bilal, hoisting his jeans. "What about Mark?"

"Nobody got hurt, thank the Lord. Mark fired one shot... guess at the monkey tryin' for you... an' all of 'em bailed their little tails. Wish I coulda seen that."

"Guess they were scared of cappin' a cop."

"They got just enough brains to be scared of that. We're still the baddest gang in town."

"So, they got away?"

"Might have been messy tryin' to stop 'em." Akeem cocked his head as his radio sputtered. "We're after the van, but 'course it was boosted. They'll probably dump it an' scatter. An' nobody saw their faces."

He glanced down the tracks at the dwindling train. The warning bells ceased at the crossing; red-and-white arms began to rise and impatient cars scuttled under. "But, you're on your way to Los Angeles now an' they ain't gonna try an' hunt you that far." He patted the Explorer's door. "What y'all think of my ride?"

"Cool." Bilal looked back at the station. "But, what about all the shit that went down? Where's Mark now?"

"Probably gettin' his ass chewed by Dobbin on the radio. Ain't lookin' forward to that myself."

"Guess I trust two cops now."

Akeem smiled. "Mark will be proud to hear that. He ain't been feelin' like much of a hero since comin' back from Iraq."

"I noticed," said Bilal. "You an' him gonna get in trouble?"

"Dobbin ain't gonna be happy we 'put the public in danger.' Like they got a right to be safe an' you don't. But he'll cover our butts. The news will call it gang-related, but it ain't gonna blow up the Dubs, losin' their victim an' runnin' away." Akeem checked his watch. "There's a steak an' eggs special at I-hop. Comes with a stack of pancakes."

"Sounds good to me." Bilal looked up at the fence. "I gotta climb that?"

"Good exercise."

Bilal wiped sweat from his face. "I just got more than I had in a year."

"Walk down to the crossin', I'll meet you." Akeem got out of his truck. "Toss me your pack."

Bilal threw it over the fence. Then he took off Devon's jacket, revealing an OPD vest. "You were right about gettin' dressed 'all the way.' Thanks."

Akeem shrugged. "We're supposed to serve an' protect. Sometimes I still believe that. ...Yo! Is that what I think it is?"

Bilal scanned the back of the jacket. "Check in my pack! Is my laptop okay?"

"Yeah," said Akeem after looking inside. "But your toothpaste got drilled. Sorry about your jacket."

"It's only a nine millimeter hole." Bilal stripped off the bulky vest and threw it over the fence to Akeem. He almost tossed the jacket, but remembered the gun in a pocket. Did he need it anymore? But he couldn't get rid of it here. And, what if Akeem got pissed at Mark for giving it to him? He donned the jacket again.

"Y'all need that on a day like this?" asked Akeem.

"I'm cool," said Bilal, scenting Devon's ghostly sweat now mingled with his own.

SIX

The sign said

RUST

and it was rusty. Ahead was a rusty iron bridge that looked about a hundred years old; and Bilal wondered if the sign was a warning, or there to call public attention to a massive example of oxidation. It was a draw-bridge, he noticed: there were two towers, one at each end, with huge iron wheels on top, and the whole center section, appar-ently, was lifted by big rusty cables. On the nearest tower, just above where the road went through, a traffic light was glowing green. Bilal supposed it would change to red when the bridge was being opened, and a wooden bar would probably close like a railroad crossing.

If the sign was a warning, the driver didn't seem to care; the bus rolled on without slowing down. Another sign said

CAUTION
STEEL DECK

Another said

TRAFFIC STOP
HERE

A fourth rusty sign on the nearest tower said something about 14 DAYS but there wasn't time to read it all. The deck was made of steel mesh so the bus almost seemed to be driving on air, and the water below was shimmering green like a jungle lagoon in a swamp-creature movie.

Bilal thought of something he'd read in a book: *burning your bridges behind you*. He supposed it meant that, if you did, you could never go back where you came from. The bus had crossed a lot of bridges since leaving Oakland hours before, but now, by crossing this rusty old bridge, a bridge that was mostly empty space like a huge skeleton of iron bones, a bridge that could open and cut off the road, it seemed like a bond had been broken somehow between his old life and what lay ahead.

Whatever that was going to be.

The bus rolled under the second tower and slowed to enter a tiny town. It had already stopped in several small towns since leaving what seemed to be a main highway and wandering into a mostly flat land of vast open fields and small groves of trees under clear blue sky and a bright yellow sun. The towns had all looked shabby and old, like parts of West Oakland scattered in Oz, though here and there were new mini-marts, fledgling strip-malls, and fast-food joints hosted by corpo-rate colonels and clowns.

But this town had none of those modern things, and nothing looked newer than the old bridge, which seemed to be its dominant feature, though probably not a tourist attraction. There were only about a dozen buildings surrounded by maybe a few dozen houses, many of which were Victorians that made Bilal think of Oakland again. The town's biggest building was rust-colored brick and might have once been a saloon or hotel, though now it was

GILMAN'S MARKET
& GENERAL MERCHANISE

according to a faded sign. Beside it was an ancient gas station with a rusty sign that said Flying Horse and pictured a weather-worn

Pegasus. There was also Zadok's Tractor repair, a little cafe named The Ideal Lunch, though visually far from idyllic, a tiny post office that looked like a jail -- built of stone, with iron-barred windows -- and some stores that seemed to be closed or abandoned, several with boards on their windows. It was like a town in a teen-slasher movie where Jason or Michael came out after dark.

The bus came to a stop with a soft hiss of brakes near the high front porch of Gilman's Market. "Rust," said the driver's voice through speakers. Like in the other little towns he didn't shut off the engine.

Bilal smiled back at Devon, then shut down and closed the Mac-Book. He wrapped it in Devon's jacket, folded the jacket into his pack, then rose from his seat and tugged up his jeans.

The driver was a big black man who looked like he'd seen every movie twice and didn't want to see one again. But he looked up as Bilal walked by and his face turned carefully kind. "Runnin' away from somethin', son?"

"...Huh?" said Bilal. "No. My cousins live here."

"Y'all sure, son? If this is as far as you could afford, I can take you on to Stockton. Our church has a shelter for kids, but we don't preach a lot an' the food ain't bad."

"...Oh," said Bilal. "Thanks. But I really do have cousins here."

The driver skinned Bilal with his eyes. "Well, this ain't West Oaktown, so 'least you won't be dodgin' bullets." Then he smiled again. "Don't get butted by a goat or step on any rattlesnakes. An' thanks for goin' Greyhound."

Bilal paused on the bus's last step as if poising on the brink of something. The air outside was hot and dry, and smelled like weeds in a vacant lot. An old pickup and a dusty car were parked in front of the little cafe, but there were no people in sight. Bilal looked back at the rusty old bridge, which had a green light on this side, too. "Is there another bus today?"

"Bored already?" chuckled the driver, his hand on the door-closing lever. "Comes though about seven-thirty tonight; 'sposed to stop but usually don't unless somebody flags it down. ...Sure you don't wanna check out our shelter? Got cable TV an' a couple computers."

"I'm cool. But thanks." Bilal stepped down to hot asphalt broken and buckled by patches of weeds like slowly invading alien life. The bus's door clunked shut behind him. The engine wound up and the bus rolled away, leaving a ghost of diesel smoke that hung in the sweltering air. He watched until the bus disappeared up the shimmering ribbon of road. Its engine sound faded and left only silence. Bilal had never heard nothing before; even at three in the morning there were semi-trucks on the 880 freeway, the rumble of trains, the scream of sirens, and usually a few gunshots.

He realized he was standing, stupidly in a parking lot, and probably *looked* like a runaway kid. There was a bench on the market's porch beneath a rusty Greyhound sign displaying an old-time silversides bus, and he climbed stone steps to sit in the shade and pulled out his cousins' address: 13 Channel Road. That couldn't be far in a town this small. He glanced at the tiny post office under a faded American flag that hung as limp as an old dishrag: this place was lucky to have a zip code! He thought about buying a Coke in the store and maybe a candy bar, but he only had twenty dollars until his grand-father sent more. Victims Assistance had helped a little, paying for part of his grandfather's move, but they'd wanted to put Bilal in a home... the System's solution to all kids' problems was snatch them away from people who loved them and lock them up with people who didn't. When Jadd Taimur had refused, the System had washed its hands of Bilal.

An elderly man came out of the store. He was white and carried a broom, and reminded Bilal of Uncle Sam, though clad in farmer overalls, a blue work shirt and a storekeeper's apron. Bilal remembered a movie about a little southern town: the man would call him a nigger and chase him off with the broom!

"Well, hello, son," said the man, with a smile.

"...Hello, sir," Bilal replied. His voice sounded white in his ears, the way he'd once talked in the North Oakland 'burbs. It surprised him to find he still knew how, but maybe it was like riding a bike.

"Don't see a lot of you folks 'round here," the old man said, still smiling.

"...Um, I guess not."

The man shifted the broom in his gnarled hands as if he was holding a rifle. "Shared a foxhole on Iwo Jima with a buddy named Leroy Washington." His faded blue eyes seemed to go far away. "I would have died for Leroy, but he ended up dyin' for me... took a Jap bayonet in the guts one night while lettin' me catch an hour of sleep. He got the Jap with his .45, but there wasn't a thing I could do for him an' the Japs got our medic the day before. Took poor Leroy a long time to die, an' I held him in my arms."

"...Oh," said Bilal. "I'm sorry."

The old man sighed. "Lotta water under that bridge. ...Need any help?"

"Do you know where Channel Road is?"

"Lookin' for the graveyard?"

"...Huh?"

The man aimed his broom at the rusty old bridge. "Right back there, this side of the channel. Runs north-east two miles past the graveyard, then dead-ends at the Dunwitch farm. ...*Used* to be the Dunwitch farm, till they sold out to the Japs like most of the other little guys. Guess the Japs won the war after all, but I still won't buy a Toyota!"

He shifted the broom. "Goin' south-west is the church, Saint Thaddeus, 'bout a half a mile." He broke into a cackle. "All the kids call it Saint Toads. Did myself when I was your age. ...Then the school, 'bout another half-mile. Then the Moonview a mile further on. Nothin' but farmland after that, till you get to Saunders Ferry, an' that's about ten miles."

His wrinkled face went sour. "Got a Walmart there. 'Bout put this town in the graveyard!"

He waved a hand across the street at several boarded buildings. "Waite's Variety went first, then Marsh's Shoes an' Allen's Rexall. Eliot's Hardware will probably go next. Barely hangin' on myself." He paused to spit off the porch. "If Walmart is 'American,' then so are all them moose-lems!"

"...Oh," said Bilal. He wondered what a Moonview was... maybe a special place to watch it? He almost asked about his cousins -- the man would probably know them since he seemed to know everything else -- but maybe he'd better stay on the low. "Thank you, sir," he said.

The man looked about to sit down with Bilal and maybe start spinning yarns, but a phone rang in the store, the old-fashioned kind with a bell. Bilal waited until he went inside, then tugged up his jeans, descended the steps and headed toward the bridge. Maybe he should go to the school? His younger cousin would probably be there, and he had to register.

SEVEN

Bilal had never walked very far – that's what busses and BART were for – but the school was only mile and he was sure he could manage that; though his back ached a little from taking the bullet -- or at least its impact -- and the weight of his pack wasn't helping. Nor was the bobbly bulk of his belly, and he had to lean backward to balance it. Thirty pounds hadn't seemed like much when living life in a static state, but this wasn't an afternoon amble with Devon up to the liquor store for snacks, or a leisurely ramble around the school track sharing Devon's punishment for the new-age sin of being "obese." The sun was hot on his arms and face, and his shirt was growing wet with sweat as he trudged along the road's dusty shoulder, where huge yellow spiders with black tiger stripes seemed to be watching from webs in tall weeds.

After maybe a quarter mile he stopped to shed his sodden shirt and put it in his pack. That cooled him off a little; and he settled into a comfortable pace, his belly rippling rhythmically, his chest orbs bobbing accompaniment and bouncing Anubis between them. Channel Road followed the river -- or was it called a channel? -- that glistened on the left-hand side. Its banks were lined with bushes and reeds in gentle shades of green, but the land was mostly open fields of dry yellow grass and brown earth tones with scattered groves of emerald oaks... the only kind of trees he knew except for weeping willows. In the distance were small rounded hills, also yellow, and dotted with oaks. He saw a big brown snake in the grass. It didn't rattle at him, but he made a wide detour around it. Should he be watching for goats? Did they sneak up on you from behind? He shot a look over his shoulder, but there was only the weathered road shimmering under the sun.

He raised his eyes to the rusty bridge towers: it didn't look like he'd come very far, though he felt like he'd walked ten miles already. Sweat now sheened his body and face, trickled hot from under his arms and leaked from his undulant cave of a navel, while droplets decorated his dreads like a dusting of glitter. His boxers were totally soaked, and his jeans growing heavy and slipping lower, puddling sloppily over his sneaks and baring an ample portion of bottom.

He continued on past a cluster of trees, and there was a shabby wooden church with a rusty bell in a tottering steeple that might have been full of slumbering bats. It looked like the church in *Jeepers-Creepers*, though in slightly better shape. He remembered an H.P. Lovecraft poem: *Beware the cracked chimes of Saint Toads.*

But a sign announced a pancake breakfast after Sunday service. Thinking of pancakes with butter and syrup reminded him of breakfast at I-hop. But that had been hours ago: he should have scored a snack at the store.

Again, he marveled how quiet it was; a transformer hummed on a telephone pole, and miles away a tractor droned across a dusty field. He thought of *Jeepers-Creepers* again and the rusty old truck the demon had driven, prowling a country road like this and piling his slaughtered victims in back. Once more he looked over his shoulder, but told himself he was watching for goats.

He glanced at the channel and thought of the gun. Akeem had bought his bus ticket, escorting him past the security guard and Greyhound's low-budget terror inspection. Once on the road, he'd jacked out the cap in the bus bathroom and loaded it back in the clip. Should he throw the gun in the water now? ...But, was he sure he wouldn't need it? A gun was no defense against demons, but what if a goat attacked?

Then he heard an engine. It sounded like a big old truck! He spun around and shed his pack, but saw an ancient muscle car, a 1970s Firebird, approaching though the haze of heat. It was trashily painted barbecue black, probably with spray cans; and its driver must have seen him and maybe wondered why he was here, because it began to slow. Bilal thought of other movies, of black people jumped by rednecks! He unzipped his pack as the car rolled up and stopped with a squeal of worn out brakes, scenting the air with hot motor oil. All the windows were open, but there was only the shirtless driver, a skinny red-haired dude of maybe seventeen, his body milk-pale and dusted with freckles as if he was spottily rusting. Death metal blasted from over-amped speakers.

The dude cut the sounds and called, "Hey, bro!"

"Hey," said Bilal, a hand on the gun in his pack.

"This the way to Saunders Ferry?"

"Um... yeah. ...About ten miles."

"Cool. Thanks." The dude took a gulp from a can of Bud. "Sorry, last one or I'd hook you up."

"That's okay," said Bilal.

"Wanna buy some kick-ass weed?"

"No thanks."

"Got some killer crystal."

Bilal frowned. "No."

"Crack?"

"No."

"Ecstasy?"

"No."

"Oxy?"

"No."

"How 'bout some old-school acid? Take a trip and never leave the farm."

"No!"

"Later, alligator." The dude popped the clutch and peeled way, spraying Bilal with gravel.

"Shit!" said Bilal. He zipped and re-shouldered his pack and started walking again.

Ahead he saw an old burger joint across the road on the riverbank. The bus had passed a lot of such places while rolling through the little towns: some, like those in West Oakland, had once been Foster Freezes or A & W Root Beers, but 'Dees, The King, and Jack In The Box had put them in the graveyard.

This place was called

THE
BURGER BARGE

but might have been a Tastee Freeze back when dinosaurs ruled. A homemade sign on a rusty pole displayed a giant cheeseburger loaded on a barge. A puffing tugboat towed the barge and looked like Little Toot. The building was made of cinder blocks, weathered white and peeling paint. A rusty awning shaded the front, and there were a dozen wooden tables, the picnic kind with benches. Bilal first thought it must be closed, aban-doned like the stores in town, but then he caught the scent of fries. And around the building were flower beds as neat as Jadd Taimur's. In the riverbank reeds behind the place was a short wooden dock and a little boat.

His stomach growled as his nose was haunted by tempting ghosts of meat and cheese. But then he saw the school ahead. He fingered Devon's charm: Devon would have bought a burger. He pictured Devon in his mind, and smiled and said, "Business first, burgers later. ...Alligator."

EIGHT

The school looked like the school in *The Birds*. It was two shabby stories of weathered white boards and stood in a weedy yellow field. To the right were rusty monkey-bars and other ancient iron things too dangerous for Oakland parks... even parks where kids were capped. To the left was a crumbling basketball court with leaning poles and netless hoops. Behind was a dusty baseball diamond, a wooden backstop and ramshackle bleachers. A faded scoreboard across the field displayed the face of a cute raccoon done in bootlegged Disney style.

RUST RACCOONS

was painted above, and the mascot's name was, naturally, Rusty.

Boys were playing flag football, while a coach who looked like a wannabe Rambo was yelling curses at them. The boys were mostly middle-school age, one team shirts, the other skins, and all streaming sweat in the blazing sun. Their shirts were the color of old life-jackets, their shorts as green as the grass should have been... Freddie Kruger colors. Most of the dudes were of pale persuasions but tanned as if they went shirtless a lot, and several were naturally brown, but nobody seemed to be black. More than a few were chubby or fat; and a pair of copper-colored boys with raven hair almost down to their waists were the fattest dudes he'd ever seen, with bellies almost reaching their knees and chests like wobbling water-balloons inflated to the verge of explosion. They were waddling slowly around a dirt track in the usual pointless purgatory for the sin of being too fat to fight other kids in a surrogate war. ...At least Bilal assumed they were boys because they didn't have shirts.

A girl's class played on the basketball court with a coach who looked like Godzilla's mom and sounded about the same. The girls were mostly white and tanned, or brown or copper like the boys, and more than a few were super-size. But, except for the sweating P.E. classes, a rusty rack of bicycles -- mostly mountain and BMX -- a few dirt-bikes and ATVs, and pickups and cars in a weedy lot, the school looked almost as dead as the town.

Bilal put on a fresh shirt from his pack – another white XXL of Devon's – mopped his face and hair with its tail, then trudged up a buckled sidewalk across a withered yellow lawn. A porcelain plaque above the doors said

RUTHERFORD RUST MEMORIAL SCHOOL 1923

which seemed to explain the name of the town and everything rusty about it. The iron door handles were half worn away from being grasped by a million kid-hands, and the hinges made a *Munsters* sound as he opened a door.

It felt hotter inside than out in the sun. There was no guard or weapons detector. The air smelled of dust, old wood and kid sweat, his own contributing to the latter. A hall ran the length of the building, and sun glared in through open back doors revealing a glimpse of the copper fat boys, who seemed to be eating candy bars as they ponderously perambulated with most of their massive bottoms bare above cartoonishly sagging shorts that only the bulk of bellies retained wallowing over mammoth thighs. ...They *had* to be boys or else this place was really strange!

The hall was higher than it was wide. Its walls were painted a bilious green like demon puke in *The Exorcist*, and lined with dented lockers, canned-pea green like Army Jeeps... at least what paint remained. The classroom door windows had wire in their glass like cop interrogation rooms, and their old-fashioned numbers were painted in gold. Dusty light fixtures like bowls of milk dangled on chains from the ceiling, but none were on and the hall was dark except for the patch of sun at the end like a light at the end of a tunnel.

To the right was a three-faucet drinking fountain, chipped, yellowed, and streaked with rust. To the left was a staircase, its treads worn in hollows. Beyond the stairs were vending machines with candy bars, chips, Hostess fruit pies, cookies, Popsicles and Coke... the newest-looking things in the house, as well as the most attractive. The usual stuff was tacked to the walls; little-kid drawings in waterpaint, all with Halloween themes, and anti-alcohol, drug, tobacco, gang, and obesity warnings... the latter apparently lame in this place, because someone had scrawled **FUCK YOU** on them.

There were two ancient posters for DARE, one still warning kids about weed... though in Bilal's experience it still made you stupid and slow. McGruff advised, "Take A Bite Out Of Crime" from somewhere back in the '80s, and a fairly new one with a skinny kid dancing -- or maybe having a spaz-attack -- proclaiming, "It's Cool To Be A Loser!"

Also boasting a big **FUCK YOU**.

There was another poster of a stereotypical cartoon bully, a big fat kid with a pit-bullish face. His belly hung out of a black T-shirt with a skull and crossbones on the front, but his arms were around two smaller boys as if they were homies in *Leave It To Beaver*. The caption said **STOP SCHOOL BULLYING**, but didn't offer any instructions on how to perform that miracle.

Bilal considered the Coke machine, but went to the drinking fountain instead to tank-up on what he'd lost on the road. On the wall above were a few pencil scrawls -- *TAD EATS BOOGERS, SWAGGART SUCKS, MARIE IS A RETARD,* and *GOAT BOY LOVES SATAN*... whatever that meant -- but nothing that looked like a gang tag.

The water was warm and tasted like tin but at least it was wet and eased his thirst. He splashed a handful on his face and dried it with his shirt. Up the hall a little way was a sign on chains that said OFFICE.

From behind closed doors came the murmur of kids and the usual droning voices of teachers, like priests reciting litanies nobody wanted to hear. He wondered if anyone else was black besides himself and his cousin, but the wire glass windows were frosty white so he couldn't see into the rooms. The only other sound was a clatter of computer keys that came from the open office door. He stopped by a case of cheap tin trophies. All were tarnished and crusted with dust, and many were projects for spiders. The newest was from a baseball game eleven years ago. If it was cool to be a loser, the Rust Raccoons could have sunk the *Titanic*.

He wondered if he should wait and register on Monday; meet his cousins, check out his new crib. And he smelled. But, that would mean walking back to town, and it didn't seem smart to be cruising around, young, black, and packing steel in a place of overwhelming white. He tugged up his jeans and entered the office.

The ceiling was high like the hallway, and bowls of milk dangled from chains. A fat pink woman who might have been fifty sat behind an Army-green desk that matched a row of file cabinets. Her computer was an ancient IMac, its keyboard as yellow as zombie teeth. A sign on the desk said Miss. Wicket, though someone had messed with the T so it looked more like a D.

A black iron fan rattled papers, but didn't make the air any cooler. The woman peered up over steel half-glasses, and the look on her face, mostly surprise, seemed to confirm Bilal's suspicion that black kids here were as rare as rust wasn't. She probably would have looked annoyed confronted by any other kid, but seemed a little uncertain of how to bully a black one. Her eyes flicked to a purse on her desk.

"...Yes?"

"Um," said Bilal and tried Devon's smile, though his voice went white as snow again. "I need to register. For eighth grade."

Again the woman looked surprised, but then recovered and scowled... something she was obviously good at. "You can't register yourself!" she snapped like he'd asked to get naked and dance. "Your parents or guardian have to do it!"

Bilal pulled an envelope out of his pack. "I'm supposed to give this to the principal."

The woman eyed him curiously, realized that, morphed back to a scowl, studied the letter suspiciously, wrinkled her nose as she caught his aroma, then glanced at a door behind her: PRINCIPAL was painted in gold across its frosted window.

"Give it to me. Sit down over there." She pointed to a wooden bench, where a million little squirming butts had probably waited for punishment. The world seemed full of nasty benches and people with attitudes at desks.

The woman took the envelope as if it might be anthrax, but seemed frustrated when she found it was sealed. She got to her feet, hesitated, then pointedly locked her purse in a drawer. Then she knocked on the principal's door, waited a moment for some sign of life, then went in, leaving it open just enough to keep an eye out for larceny.

Bilal was tired but stayed on his feet. He glanced at a fly-specked clock on the wall, surprised to see it was almost 2:30. That triggered a growl in his belly: he should have bought a burger, as Devon would have done.

More posters hung on the demon-puke walls, including the blubbery bully and friends. He noticed a dusty painting of a big fat man in an old-fashioned suit who looked like Uncle Fester. On the frame was a tarnished brass tag: Rutherford Runcible Rust.

A moment later the woman returned looking more curious than ever. "Go in," she commanded, stepping aside as if Bilal might be contagious.

NINE

The principal's office was even hotter; demon-spew green with a milk-bowl light and reeking of old tobacco smoke. Another antique iron fan rattled papers like dead autumn leaves but only blew the heat around. Two tall windows were open, the sunlight filtered through rust-colored shades and giving the room a moldy glow. From outside came the squeals of girls and the bawls of the coach cursing boys. A bony white man who looked like the preacher in *Poltergeist II* sat behind another green desk. His face was skullish with long gleam-ing teeth behind lips that didn't seem able to close, and his white dress shirt looked old and yellowed like something dug up from a crypt... or maybe it was only the light.

He was tightening his tie as Bilal came in, his hands like twitching corpse's claws. On his desk was a butt-filled ashtray, and a smog of smoke hazed the sultry air despite the rattling fan. He studied Bilal from deep-set eyes that looked like empty sockets. It was hard for a skull to look curious -- or much of anything else -- but this one didn't look happy. The bony hands gripped Bilal's letter, open on the desk top. A hollow voice said, "Close the door, Mr. ...Taimur. Did I pronounce that correctly?"

"Yea... yes, sir," said Bilal.

A skeletal finger pointed. "Please sit down. You may remove your pack if you wish. My name is Mr. Skelly."

Bilal wondered if the man was joking, but decided he wasn't. "Hi. Thanks." His voice came out white but he couldn't stop it. He closed the door behind him, glimpsing the woman, who looked disappointed, then shrugged off his pack and sat down on a chair that felt like an alien torture device. At least the raging tobacco reek would mask his own sweaty scent.

Mr. Skelly regarded the letter and cleared his throat with a death-rattle sound. "I've already gotten an email from the principal of your former school. He said you've been a good student." The empty sockets scanned Bilal as if trying to X-ray his oversize shirt. "Though your grades in physical-fitness leave a lot to be desired. Still, I'm impressed by your other grades... though your school may have lower standards than mine." He looked a little uncomfortable... pretty hard for a skull to do. "You've been in trouble with the law?"

"No, sir," said Bilal. "I got in trouble because of the law." He smiled like Devon again. "I tried to take a bite out of crime, but it bit me back."

The skull looked not amused. "I hope you don't have an attitude problem."

Bilal wasn't sure how to answer that. "I'm hoping to go to college."

"...Good," said the skull, though seeming surprised. "What are you planning to study?"

"Horror movie filmography. I wanna do FX."

"...FX?"

"Special Effects. Like ghosts and... monsters." Bilal had almost said skeletons, and Mr. Skelly was his own FX.

"...Interesting," said the skull. "I'm pleased to hear you have goals. So many young people today just drift through life like..."

"Ghosts in a graveyard?" suggested Bilal before he thought about it.

"...An interesting simile. ...Do you know what a simile is?"

"A metaphor with 'like' in front."

"Good. So you realize the importance of studying hard and apply-ing yourself. Thinking about your future. ...And staying out of trouble."

"Yes, sir."

Mr. Skelly opened a drawer and took out a big brown envelope. "Your transfer arrived yesterday, but I must say this is unusual. ...At least in this school district. We don't have these kinds of... problems... here. And we certainly don't want them."

"I didn't want them myself," said Bilal.

The skull seemed to listen for attitude, then maybe decide it hadn't heard any. "Your principal didn't give any details about the nature of your... problem. But I understand the police were involved?"

"Yes, sir," said Bilal. "But I'm not supposed to talk about it. I guess you could call OPD."

"Who?" asked Mr. Skelly.

"Oakland Police Department. Maybe Detective Dobbin."

"I have." The skull looked annoyed. "He wasn't very helpful. But, I assume it's for your safety. In other words, you've been a victim?"

Bilal frowned but nodded.

The skull looked uncomfortable again. "You're a Muslim?" he asked, pronouncing it moose-lem.

"...Sorta," said Bilal.

"What do you mean?"

"...Well..." Bilal said carefully. "Are you a Christian, sir?"

The skull pondered that for a moment. "I do believe in a... higher power, though I don't believe it lives in a church or requires a priest to find it. But I thought your religion was... a bit more strict."

Bilal smiled. "Like, 'Anyone who works on the Sabbath must be put to death?'"

The skull looked startled. "Is that in the Quran?"

"No, sir, the Bible. But maybe it's a metaphor."

"...I... may see your point," said the skull. "But, your religion has nothing to do with your... problem?"

"No, sir," said Bilal.

Mr. Skelly glanced at the door, where a shadow had darkened the glass. He flicked a switch on an old intercom that looked like something from Frankenstein's lab. "Miss. Wicket? Will you get me a cup of coffee, please?" He waited until the woman replied with a scratchy cat sound from the speaker, then turned to Bilal again. "By state and federal regulations we shouldn't be talking about religion. If you'd rather not..."

"That's coo... okay," said Bilal.

The skull seemed to ponder again. "This is a small rural school in a small rural community where people generally get along. As you may have noticed it's mostly... white... though many farm workers are Hispanic. We also have a few Ori... Asians, and there is a small reservation of Native-Americans. I'm not prejudiced, Mr. Taimur... of religion or of race... and I want you to know you can trust me."

"Thank you, sir," said Bilal, while thinking of burrahobbits.

Mr. Skelly slipped Bilal's letter into the big envelope, put the envelope into a drawer and locked it with a rusty key... which seemed a bit overdramatic. "I don't want to know what your problem was. And no one else here will know you had one." He looked uncomfortable again. "And, no one *has* to know..." He cleared his throat. "Not that I'm suggesting..."

The skull looked very unhappy now. "You don't openly practice... Islam? Praying all day and... that sort of thing."

"Not for awhile," said Bilal. "Since my parents..." He stopped then said, "Which makes my grandfather sad."

The skull looked relieved. "My mother was religious. ...Not *fanatical,* of course. But she may have felt like your grandfather does when I stopped attending church in my teens."

"I think I understand," said Bilal.

"Are you questioning your faith?"

"I'm questioning lot of things."

"That's perfectly normal at your age. ...You don't object to Christmas? We have a school tree and a manger scene."

Bilal shrugged. "I always gave my friend a present, an' he always gave me one. That kinda stuff makes people happy. Christmas trees an' Easter eggs. Ramadan an' Kwanza. Only a stupid hater would try an' make trouble for people who like them."

"That's a very tolerant point of view. One should always be tolerant of other people's differences. But, regardless of religion, you're our first African-American student. And that, of course, is obvious."

Now it was Bilal who looked startled. He almost asked about his cousin... but maybe it was best to stay cool?

"As I said," the skull went on, "I'm not in the least prejudiced. I served in Vietnam with many... of your people... and came to like and trust them, often with my life. But neither am I a Pollyanna. ...Do you know what that means?"

"Um," said Bilal. "Someone who thinks everybody is good if you give 'em a chance?"

The skull almost smiled, though Bilal was glad it didn't. "I doubt if many students here would know the definition." But then it frowned as the boys' coach yelled, "Move it, you fat blanket-asses!" Whatever that meant. Finally it studied Bilal again. "You seem like an intelligent young man so I won't put a candy coating on this. Problems often follow your people."

He rose and went to the windows, his gaunt shape stark against the sun as he raised a shade and looked out... a skeleton waiting for sunset to go and haunt somebody. "Rust may not be a pretty town, at least aesthetically. ...Do you know what that means?"

"How it looks?" said Bilal, thinking of candy and wishing he'd bought some.

"Good," said Mr. Skelly. "But, while we have a few minor problems... underage drinking, a bit of 'weed'... there is no gang violence or crack in this town, and many people still don't lock their doors. There hasn't been a... murder... here since 1933. The people may seem a bit 'slow' compared to those you're accustomed to... maybe not very 'hip' or 'down with what's up'... but they all have eyes in their heads and they see when something isn't right. ...Such as drugs or crime." He dropped the shade and faced Bilal. "Do we understand each other?"

Bilal's voice slipped back to normal... at least what he'd thought was normal. "People are gonna be watchin' me to see if I'm a monkey."

"...A...? That sounds like attitude."

"No, sir, it's a metaphor."

"...I see," said Mr. Skelly, though he obviously didn't. He returned to his desk, and Bilal expected a clicking sound as his bony butt met the unpadded chair. "I'll have Miss. Wicket type your schedule and give you a copy of our rules." He scanned Bilal's jeans. "Which include a dress code. ...May I ask you to raise your shirt?"

Bilal pulled his shirt up to his neck, the orbs of his chest spilling flubberly free.

"No looser or lower than that." The skull did smile, which looked even scarier than Bilal had imagined. "No pants on the ground in my turf, dog."

"Yes, sir."

"I hope you're not becoming obese. You could lose a little weight."

And you should gain a ton! thought Bilal. "I'm also tolerant of size."

"...Yes," said the skull. "It's easy to forget size discrimination in a culture where health is important."

"Or just looks?" suggested Bilal. He realized his white voice was useful; it seemed to make people think he was smart. "We're taught some looks are better than others, even if they're not."

"...Well... unfortunately that's true." Mr. Skelly seemed to sigh. "But the new state guidelines mandate weight control education, so I'm forced to at least make a comment, though please understand I'm not 'dissing' you."

"No problem," said Bilal.

The coach's voice hollered again, "You got tits like a girl, you want ovaries, too?"

The skull really sighed. "Back to the matter at hand: no graphic T-shirts with violent, obscene, or hateful motifs."

"Yes, sir."

"Graffiti is an instant suspension... I assume you call it 'tagging?'"

"Yes, sir."

"May I ask what you're wearing around your neck?"

"Anubis."

"Is that an Islamic symbol? ...Not that I mind, since many Hispanic students wear crosses."

"No, sir, it's Egyptian, and they had a whole bunch of gods."

"Why do you wear it?"

"It belonged to my friend. ...He's dead."

"...Oh... I'm sorry. But, nothing to do with gangs?"

"Not the necklace, sir."

"Any... er, tattoos?"

Bilal felt Devon's smile again. "No, sir." Then he added

innocently as Devon might have done, "I can take off my clothes if you wanna check."

That got past the attitude radar and Mr. Skelly looked startled. "That won't be necessary. But, of course you'll be dressing down for P.E."

"Yes, sir."

"Our school gym clothes are thirty dollars... thirty-five for triple-X... and Gilman's Market has them. ...But if you need financial assistance..."

"I might," said Bilal. He thought about the long-haired boys, who might have paid fifty for only their shorts.

"I'll make a note of that. ...No wireless phone use during school hours."

"I don't have one," said Bilal.

"And, of course no weapons or firearms."

"Of course," said Bilal, though Devon-like tempted to ask if that only meant use.

"Our lunch is two dollars a day... and assistance is available."

"That's coo... okay," said Bilal.

"Good. And there are vending machines in the hall. Their proceeds help maintain our school."

"You got a lot of good stuff."

"*Have* a lot of good stuff."

"Yes, sir."

"Of course the students' likes and dislikes determine the selections."

"Nobody ate fruit at my school either, unless it was a roll-up."

"...Our students are normal, too. And, this is a closed campus." Mr. Skelly smiled like a nightmare. "No sneaking out to the Burger Barge... but the Tugboat Triple 'rocks.'"

"...Yes, sir."

In the distance, down the road, a hoarse iron bell clanked three times. *Beware the cracked chimes of Saint Toads*, thought Bilal.

Mr. Skelly glanced at his watch. "Since we're halfway through last period, it might be more convenient if you started on Monday."

"Yes, sir."

"Very well, Mr. Taimur." The skull extended a grisly hand. "Welcome to Rutherford Rust Memorial."

Bilal took the hand, which felt like bones in a paper towel. "Thank you, sir."

"By the way," said the skull as Bilal got his pack and turned to leave. "I'm sure Coach Swaggart would welcome you on our basketball team."

"I'm not very good at sports," said Bilal.

The skull looked disappointed.

TEN

The afternoon air was even hotter. Bilal stripped off his shirt again when back on the road to Rust, and was gleaming like polished obsidian by the time he neared the Burger Barge, which didn't look like the kind of place where shirts were required for service. The enticing aromas of burgers and fries ghosted above the smells of hot asphalt, sun-drenched earth, and the steamy scent of the green channel water. A semi-truck sat in the dirt parking lot, its engine idling smoke from the stack. Its double trailers were loaded with hay bales that towered over the truck itself like the giant cheeseburger dwarfed the tug. A white guy who looked like a cowboy was sitting at one of the tables with a bottle of Bud and a big juicy burger, while *Truckin'* by The Grateful Dead bumped from an old Seeburg jukebox. The man glanced up as Bilal walked by, but didn't seem to see any "problems."

Bilal went to the order window and scanned the menu board. Inside, among the milkshake machine, softee dispenser and bubbling deep-fryer, a big brawny woman was scraping the grill. She was clad in a grease-spattered apron, faded Levis, white T-shirt, and a battered-looking captain's cap. She had iron-gray hair and a weathered bronze face, and was smoking a nasty little cigar that looked like a piece of Slim Jim and smelled like burning a brown paper bag. She smiled when she saw him and came to the counter, wiping her hands on a dishrag. "What'll it be, my man?"

"My man" sounded cool, if prehistoric; and Bilal's belly growled as he studied the menu. "Um, what's good?"

The big woman boomed out a laugh. "Ain't nothin' not good in my galley, son! But you ain't gonna find no 'healthy' crap here. No

58

tofu burgers or vegetable dogs, or something that looks like a dung-beetle rolled it onto your plate. An' nothin' that's only 'light' on taste or pretending to be what it wished it was. Just real honest food like I grew up eatin'. I'm seventy-four, wanna arm wrestle?"

Bilal smiled. "I'm sure you could beat me."

The woman's voice was deep and rough as if she had yelled a lot in her life, and the blue of her eyes was startling in the old-penny tan of her face. "Just passin' through?"

"I... might be gonna live here awhile. Just registered at school."

"Meet the skull?" asked the woman.

"Yeah."

"Ol' Skelly could give the Grim Reaper night terrors, but he ain't a bad guy an' he runs a good school. Rust Raccoons never win any games, but kids learn the three Rs better than most an' that seems to make 'em pretty good people. An' Rust itself ain't a bad little town. What's left of it, anyhow."

She turned to gaze at the sun-shimmered channel. "Been all up an' down the Delta. Ran a tug for forty years. Wanted me a place on the water where I could watch the tows go by." She blew out a cloud of smoke. "But, ain't much passin' here no more 'cept people fishin' an' cruisin' houseboats." She frowned at the cowboy-driver. "Trucks took over most of the freight, an' dredging the channel ain't 'green.' 'Sposed to be bad for salamanders who ain't got the brains to evolve. Bridge ain't opened but twice this year, 'cept for monthly testin'. Nothin' big to open it for."

"Guess you been here a long time," said Bilal.

"Seen a lot of kids grow up. Never had time to make none of my own, an' now it's a little too late." She thrust a hand over the counter. "Name's Annie, but you're too young to get the joke."

"Bilal," said Bilal, shaking Annie's hefty hand.

"Glad to meet you, Bilal. My engineer was black an' we never had a breakdown." Annie boomed another laugh. "Guess you could call it black power. Wish I coulda married that man but he was already taken. The good ones always are."

"Are there any black people in Rust?" asked Bilal.

"One in the graveyard. ...Most of him."

"...Huh?"

"Used to be the bridge tender." Annie glanced at the rusty old bridge down the channel a mile away. "Hoist gear jammed an' then let go while he was tryin' to clear it. Sliced his head clean off his shoulders, an' nobody ever found it! Nice fella, too, everyone liked him. Most of the town showed up for his funeral... closed coffin, of course."

Bilal felt confused: Jadd Taimur had told him his uncle had died -- in an accident on a bridge -- but what about his cousins?

"Was he a relation?" asked Annie. "Sorry about the head if he was."

Bilal hesitated: it was hard to be sad about somebody's head when you'd never known the person inside. Dobbin had warned him to be careful of who he talked to and what he said. It had taken hours to get here on a bus that stopped in every town big enough to have a name, but Oakland wasn't far away; probably less than an hour by car.

"No," he said. And maybe it wasn't a lie... he didn't know for sure. "So, what's really good? Like, hot an' a lot for a Lincoln or less?"

"Try the Tugboat Triple," said Annie. "Three big juicy patties of god-honest beef, three kinds of cheese an' all the fixin's. Special comes with Swab Bucket Fries an' a tanker size Coke."

"Right on," said Bilal.

Bells jangled back at the school as he took a seat at one of the tables. He watched as the doors burst open and kids poured out like a rowdy river. A lot of boys instantly lost their shirts as if reverting to wild things, and forbidden phones were clamped to ears. Many kids went to the bicycle rack, where nothing seemed to be locked. Others mounted dirt-bikes, kicking starters and revving engines, while others fired-up ATVs. Across the road was a dock like Annie's, and several kids got into boats, pulling starters and whooshing away. More kids boarded an old yellow bus, while others just walked down the road.

Like the gym classes he'd seen on the field, most of the kids were ethnically white, though Hispanics were well represented; and there were some copper kids who must have been Native-American, most of them chubby or brazenly fat, and all boasting long raven hair as if proud of their heritage. He also noticed a handful of Asians.

But, where was his cousin? ...Maybe he schooled online? Or, maybe he went to a private school? Maybe even a Muslim school... there was probably one in Stockton, not too far away. But, Annie had been here for years and seemed to know all about the place, and said she hadn't seen any black kids. Muslims probably weren't popular here with all the hate and ignorance ranted online and spewed from TV: the storekeeper thought they were worse than Walmart, and the skull had advised him to stay on the under... at least without actually saying so. But, the bridge tender had been well-liked. ...He *had* to have been Bilal's uncle; a black man killed in a bridge accident couldn't have been a coincidence.

Maybe he'd converted to whatever went to Saint Toads? Ate pancake breakfasts after prayer and never had to fast? Or, maybe he'd just rejected religion and done the right thing on his own? Married -- maybe -- and raised two kids. Become a part of this little town. So, maybe his cousins weren't Muslim?

But, they still had to be black.

Bilal tried to figure things out: had his cousins moved since their father was killed? ...But, Jadd Taimur had written to them in Rust only a week ago.

He pulled the address from his pocket, blurry because of his sweat: 13 Channel Road.

He suddenly felt very alone. What should he do if his cousins weren't here? Catch a Greyhound back to Oakland? Then what? He didn't know where his grandfather was, and wouldn't know until Jadd Taimur wrote. He could stay with Devon's mom, but that would mean going back to the 'hood. ...And putting her in danger.

He could run to the cops, but they would lock him up somewhere, even if they called it a home.

Akeem had given Bilal his cop card along with his email and home phone number. Akeem and Mark would help him... but they had already risked their jobs, not to mention their lives, to get him safely here.

He shoved the paper back in his pocket. He wasn't a scared little kid! He'd done what any good *man* would do; he should be acting like a man, thinking of others instead of himself.

He felt a gentle urge to pray, like his grandfather's hand on his shoulder, to ask for Allah's guidance… and maybe His forgiveness for questioning his faith.

Annie's voice boomed from the window: "Tugboat Triple Special!"

Bilal had turned toward the east, away from the brassy afternoon sun. It said in the Quran that Allah's mercy prevailed over His anger… but maybe Bilal had to earn that mercy instead of just asking for it?

Again he felt an urge to pray, but instead grasped Devon's necklace, picturing Devon across the table waiting for a triple cheeseburger. "Tell me what to do, man."

ELEVEN

Bilal took his food to the farthest table under the rusty awning's shade overlooking the little boat dock in the reeds. He shed his pack before sitting down, then unwrapped the monster burger, a triple tower of meat and cheese that started a party in his mouth as soon as he took the first juicy bite. The golden fries were home-style, crispy on the outside, tender in the center, and seasoned to per-fection.

The cowboy-driver dropped his trash in a rusty, topless oil drum and mounted his idling steed. Air brakes hissed and the truck rumbled off with its tottering trailers of hay. Kids from school began to arrive, the bratty dirt-bikes snarling in first and skidding up dust in sideways stops, followed by foot-powered BMX bikes that copied the motorized moves. Most of the riders were shirtless, and none wore safety helmets.

A pair of ATVs roared up, driven by the super-size dudes who Bilal had seen at the school. They seemed to be twins, and were even more awesomely fatter up close. Though maybe only seventh-graders, and a head shorter than Bilal, they were easily four times as big around, almost as wide as they were tall, their huge hips and bottoms straining old jeans that seemed more like decorations than clothes, their bellies mammoth masses of blubber cascading over gargantuan thighs, their chests looking even more like balloons pumped to the edge of exploding. Their cheeks engulfed small button noses; their eyes were only obsidian slits; and their lips were cute rosebuds like Chucky's but lacking the evil expression.

Other boys and girls rolled up on mountain bikes and cruisers, followed by the kids on foot. The bigger dudes, seventh and eighth graders, naturally got to order first, some escorting girlfriends. A few of the kids glanced at Bilal, but like the cowboy-driver didn't seem to see any "problems."

He noticed some of the younger boys looking nervously back at the school like kids in Oakland alert for a drive-by. Then he heard an iron chugging that sounded like a big lawnmower, and down the road from the school parking lot came an old dinosaur of a minibike. It had twelve-inch tires worn half bald, a frame that looked like water pipe, and was either painted faded orange or maybe only rusty. Its huge one-cylinder engine looked like something powered by steam and was guarded by heavy steel mesh. Its tiny headlight had no lens, only a bulb with a tarnished reflector, and looked like a tunafish can. Its chain was loose and rattling, and it farted a trail of oily blue smoke.

Two boys were riding the ancient machine. The driver looked like a visual joke, like the rusty RUST sign at the rusty old bridge. Hallo-ween was still a few days away so he probably wasn't in costume, but he could have been the poster-boy for the Stop School Bullying cartoon. In fact, he looked like the cartoon bully in *Cree-show II*. His blubber-bulked arms were massive in a black T-shirt three sizes too small and straining skin-tight over bulbous breasts that seemed to be daring anyone to suggest they didn't belong to a boy. The rolls of his waist bulged out on each side, while his belly poured over the bike's gas tank as if he was packing a pillow. He wore old jeans with one ripped knee, their cuffs in ribbons like zombie rags, his butt mostly bare on the bike's leather seat; and his feet were clad in motocross boots about the size of Frankeinstein's with brutally steel-armored toes. What might have been a pit-bull's chain was wrapped around one of the boots, and another chain tethered his wallet to a steel-studded black leather belt. On both chubby wrists were spiked fighting cuffs; on eight chubby fingers were heavy brass rings with colored glass stones -- red, green, yellow and blue -- the kind that kids in the 1960s had ordered from comic book ads. They had been advertised as "stunning"... and were if you punched somebody. His double-chinned face with chipmunk cheeks was set in a looking-for-trouble snarl, and a cigarette hung from one side of his mouth. His hair was black and curly, tumbling over brawny shoulders and totally hiding his eyes above a wide snubby nose. His face and arms looked more dirty than tanned, a sort of dusky indefinite shade, though the underside of his belly was pale where it couldn't be touched by the sun.

Bilal thought of fat Italian kids like gangsters' sons in movies, stuffing down pizza in smoky back rooms while their fathers planned hits and extortion. But, whatever he ethnically was, he was big, a few inches taller than Bilal and easily twice the weight. He'd be slow in a fight but hard to hurt with all that fat for armor. And those rings and spikes would leave nasty wounds.

The boy at his back made a stark contrast; a fair and flawless *Elfquest* male who could have been a living Cutter, coppery tanned, with blue Bambi eyes. His silky hair was pale gold and flowed in ripples midway down his back; and he wore big-jeans as loose and low as Mr. Skelly allowed, their cuffs hiding all but the toes of his sneakers. His blue-and-white checkered shirt was unbuttoned, displaying a six-pack and high-jutting pecs, though he looked toylike behind the fat dude and was probably six inches shorter. There wasn't much room on the minibike's seat, and his own tight bottom hung half off the back, his arms around the blubbery boy.

A bully usually had a posse, and another boy pedaled an old BMX behind the chugging minibike. He also fronted a cigarette snarl but wasn't smoking tobacco.

Bilal had never seen a goat except in movies and on TV, but this dude actually looked like one! Bilal remembered a Lovecraft story about an evil "goatish boy" who'd terrorized a town. The dude had an almost chinless face with a nearly bridgeless puggy nose. His eyes were narrow and slanted, and a strange yellow shade, while his two front teeth were alarmingly large, aimed in opposite directions and might have opened bottlecaps. His tangled brown hair was shoulder-length and oily as a junkyard dog's. He was probably twelve, thirteen at most, but his cheeks and jaw were fuzzy with down, including a smudge above his lip, while his forearms were actually furry. His body was chubby and boyishly-breasted in a loosely lazy-kid way with pouches of fat squeezed under his arms, but his belly was huge dispropor-tionately, ballooning out of a rat-colored 'beater that once upon a time had been white, hanging like a bag of blubber over the bike's upper frame and lolling side-to-side as he pedaled.

Bilal remembered a picture he'd seen of a goat boy playing a flute in a forest. ...Weren't they called fauns? The only thing missing was horns on his head, but maybe, like Hellboy, he'd cut them off.

The minibike chugged to a dust-swirling stop with a teeth-gritting squeal from its rear wheel brake. The fat dude killed the engine by grounding out the spark plug and dropped the stubby kickstand. He peered around like a predator, though Bilal wondered how he could see: if his nose had been black and shiny he would have looked like a fat sheepdog.

His blond companion slid off the seat and posed with hands on narrow hips. His shirt spread open to show off his chest, while his saggers slipped illegally low displaying six inches of snowy-white shorts. He was spotless compared to the other two boys, his clothes all clean and fairly new, including his big high-top kicks.

"Goat Boy" rolled up on his BMX, dropped the bike in the powdery dust and tried to strike a pose like the blond, though he had to lean backward to balance his belly, which, since he was now vertical, pendulously overhung dirty jeans, their cuffs puddled over tattered sneaks, which were cartoonishly monsterous... maybe to conceal cloven hooves?

The bully dismounted his minibike, his belly hanging way out of his shirt, as if winning a competition with "Goat Boy," his navel a smile upside-down. An old song bumped from the jukebox: Bilal always pictured a Kid Bop vid whenever he heard that tune; a bunch of third-graders howling, *"Welcome to the jungle, baby, now you're gonna diiiiiie!"*

The older dudes and their girlfriends had gotten their food and were sitting at tables, talking and eating, yacking on phones. Several had fired cigarettes, and tobacco smoke mingled with scents of meat, fresh salty fries and hot melted cheese. Only the younger boys looked wary, watching the bully and posse like sheep would watch invading wolves. Several had left the order line and were edging toward their bikes. A skinny sixth-grader reached his cruiser.

"You!" yelled Goat Boy, his voice like a bleat. He swaggered up to the smaller kid in a comical backward-leaning gait. "Get me a Tugboat Triple! Swab Bucket Fries an' a Tanker Coke! ...No, make it a shake... vanilla!"

The younger boy sighed and went back to the line.

"Give him firsts!" ordered Goat Boy, and the other kids shuffled aside. Bilal remembered the pencil tag above the drinking fountain at school: *Goat Boy Loves Satan*. This could have been a son of Satan put on earth to practice.

The bully was scanning around, taking his time choosing a victim. His unseen eyes beneath his hair seemed to find Bilal and lock.

Shit! thought Bilal. That was all he needed! To get in a fight on his first day here and make a debut as a "problem!" Could he put the dude on his back without a major production? But, what about his dogs? Goat Boy wasn't much of a threat, small, stoned, and marshmallow fat, but the muscular blond would be fast. Bilal thought of the gun, but that was stupid! Better to submit like a Beta than pull the steel and go to prison like a monkey-boy.

He could feel those hidden eyes probably trying to rate him. Despite the myths in Disney movies, not all bullies were closet cowards who backed away from real fights or someone standing up to them. But then the dude turned away. He seemed a little uncertain, but maybe he didn't want to fight when there was lots of easy prey? He walked with a swaggering waddle, the jingle and clink of his chains sounding like spurs in a cowboy movie. The blond boy followed as quiet as cats, while Goat Boy also shuffled along, maybe for work-experience. The bully stepped to the Indian twins, who'd ponderously gotten off their machines and, wobbling and rippling everywhere, each an earthquake in coppery Jell-O, had reached the end of the order line, although it seemed like a miracle, or at least a defiance of some law of phyics, that they could even manage to walk.

"Your turn, blanket-asses," bully boy growled. "Tugboat Triples for me an' Shawn. Big fries, Cokes, an' blueberry sundaes."

The twins looked resigned in stereo and jiggled to join Goat Boy's victim. The other younger boys had chilled, beginning to grin and goof around like everything was cool again: the lion had made his kill so the rest of the antelope were safe. At least until tomorrow.

Bilal went back to work on his burger… a very savory labor of love. At least he knew what blanket-ass meant. He'd finish his food, go back to town and check out his cousins' address. If they had moved he'd call Akeem.

A group of maybe a dozen boys came jogging down the road from the school, clad in gym shorts and dusty sneaks, and plodding in that weary way of kids with many miles to go and no reward for getting there. They ranged from skinny to borderline fat, a few equipped with moderate muscles, which seemed to exemplify the finest of physical fitness in Rust – except for "Elf Boy," who had his own planet -- but all were panting and pouring sweat and looked like a bunch of tortured souls being herded to hell by a demon... in this case the coach in Freddy's track suit who cruised behind in a topless Jeep.

"Don't even think about it, *girls!*" he yelled as the boys slowed their pace to wistfully gaze at the kids drinking Cokes. "We're gonna *win* this year if I have to kick all your fat asses to do it!" He looked like he wished he had a whip, and bellowed at the chubbiest boy, who was naturally plodding last. "Move it, piggy! ...All of you run like little gay boys!" He almost rammed the chubby kid, but then cut close to the parking lot. "Shawn!" he yelled to the elf. "It's not too late to get back on the team! We can *beat* Saunders Ferry this year!"

The blond boy flipped an elvish El Birdo.

The coach's face flashed rosy red, but he and his panting prisoners went on, plodding down the road to Rust. Bilal returned to his burger. He heard the metallic jingle again and watched the bully swagger past from under lowered lashes. A haze of boy-sweat, grungy jeans, engine oil and cigarette smoke smogged the air around him. He kept his eyes down as the blond boy passed; only the rustle of dragging cuffs and maybe a whiff of Brut. Then Goat Boy. Bilal had read that goats smelled bad, but Goat Boy might have smelled bad to a goat. Besides rank sweat and dirty clothes, there was also a randy seminal scent overtopping the reek of cheap middle-school weed.

Bully and posse trooped out on the dock toting their extorted food and losing their shirts before sitting down. The blond boy looked even more like Cutter with all his pretty muscles displayed. The fat dude might have been Kung Fu Panda, while Goat Boy looked like a failed experiment of crossing a kid with a flabby Teenwolf and overfeeding the nasty result.

The human kids were leaving, mounting bikes and kicking starters, the Indian twins on their ATVs. They must have had plenty of wampum because each had ordered Tugboat Triples after treating Bully and friend.

Other kids walked away down the road after tossing their trash in the oil drum. Annie was cleaning up inside, polishing the shake machine and singing a song about rolling in clover that wouldn't be on the Kid Bop chart.

The bell of Saint Toads clanked four times, and Bilal was downing the last of his fries when a 4X4 pickup, a hooptie nineteen-something Dodge, rattled into the parking lot. Its bed was loaded with hay bales, its battered body caked with dust. A Guns 'N Roses sticker adorned its cracked windshield, and its stereo blasted a Def Leppard song. The driver and his two companions looked like shirtless tenth-graders, white, tanned and wiry, all with '80s rocker hair. The dudes got out like regulators. One went to the minibike and kicked it over, which seemed to explain their mission. Then they headed for the dock, barely giving Bilal a glance and raising dust as they passed. Bilal gulped the last of his Coke. This would be a wise time to leave. Maybe Rust didn't have gangs, but there seemed to be plenty of teen terrorists.

TWELVE

Bilal was gathering up his trash as the last of the other kids left. The jukebox ended another song and everything got quiet again. A gang of crows came flapping down to gobble bits of burger buns and scraps around the tables. The three big dudes had reached the dock. One, a blond and slenderly ripped, stabbed a finger at the elf. "I told you not to hang with him!"

Elf Boy leaped to his feet. "You ain't the boss of me!"

They were obviously brothers, and the big one yelled, "Get in the truck! ...NOW, asshole! Or I'm tellin' mom an' dad!"

Bully Boy also got up. His blond companion hesitated, but Bully said, "It's cool, go on."

"But..."

"Go on, man." Bully spit at one of the bigger boys' sneaks, missing by less than an inch. "I ain't scared of these dorks!"

The elf-kid glared at the big boys. "That's what you are!"

"GET THE FUCK IN THE TRUCK!" bawled his brother.

The elf hesitated again, but finally stalked away up the dock.

"Hey, goat boy!" yelled another big dude. "We don't wanna beat up a retarded freak, but you better take off or you're gonna get owned!"

Goat Boy had also risen, barring his bottle-opener teeth and clenching furry fists, though any one of the bigger dudes could have dropped him with a slap. But Bully said, "Go home, Jody."

Jody looked like he wanted to stay -- which meant he either had super-size balls, or maybe he *was* retarded -- but also reluctantly left, cartoonishly in his huge dragging jeans.

Bilal remained at the table, not wanting to attract attention by making any moves. Elf Boy passed him muttering curses, climbed in the truck and slammed the door as if trying to break the glass. Goat Boy also passed Bilal, fouling the air again with funk, hopped his bike and headed for town. Bilal knew he should vacate, too; the scene on the dock was way too familiar, the three big dudes and their cornered victim. He'd seen this shit a thousand times in schoolyards, parks, in alleys and streets.

Still, he stayed at the table. He wondered why he couldn't leave: the fat boy was a bully. Why should he care if a bully got beat? *As ye sow, so shall ye reap* as it said in Akeem's Bible, or *No one will reap except what they sow*, as the Quran put it.

He reached for his pack to put it on, but left it where it lay. His eyes went back to the dock... it was like a typical teen-slasher flick where some dim-witted dork went down to the basement no matter how stupid that was.

This bully wasn't a closet coward. He stood like a fat young lion at bay facing a pack of tigers. He should have looked ridiculous, his eyes still covered by his hair, his belly wobbling with his breaths, but there was a threat in those blubber-bulked arms, backed by the rings and those wicked spiked cuffs. The three big dudes stepped carefully, predators knowing their prey could bite.

Real fights never looked like movies; things happened fast with no camera angles or long dramatic slow-motion shots. The bully was fast for a fat kid, but painfully slow compared to the others. Knocking over a Tanker Coke, he landed a fist on Elf Boy's brother, his rings smashing into the dude's jaw with a meaty thud that made Bilal wince. The dude backed away and cursed, and, had it only been two against one, the bully might have had a chance; but the other big boys grabbed him, scattering half-eaten burgers and fries while pinning his arms behind his back. The first dude, jaw bleeding from Bully Boy's rings, began a methodical beat-down, though he didn't look very experienced, wast-ing a lot of body punches, his fists only bouncing off blubber, but he had all the time in the world, and who was going to stop him.

Bilal knew it was stupid -- the same kind of stupid that had screwed up his life and almost gotten his grandfather killed -- but he was tired of being a witness to everything wrong in the world! A good man *did* something when bad things happened, he didn't just sit on his ass and watch and then pretend he hadn't seen! He jumped to his feet and ran to the dock. Halfway there he remembered the gun. Was he stupid to leave it? Or would he be stupider to bring it?

The two dudes pinning Bully Boy were facing the shore and saw him coming. Their faces mirrored surprise. It took a second before one yelled, "Chris, look out!"

Elf Boy's brother spun around in time to get Bilal's sneak in his crotch. He screamed like a girl and clutched himself, crashing down on the splintery boards, his face smooshing into a blueberry sundae. One of the other boys cursed. Bilal expected the N-word but got the F one instead. The dude let go of Bully, cocked his fists and came at Bilal. Bully Boy, gasping, streaming sweat, saw his chance and used his mass, bucking back on the boy holding him. The dude lost his balance, then his grip, and toppled into the water with a spectacular splash.

The other big dude swung at Bilal, but had no moves and Bilal dodged away. Doubling his fists, Bilal swung hard, slamming the dude in the stomach. Bully Boy kicked the dude's knee from behind. That *was* a move and the boy flipped backwards, crashing down on the boards. The boy in the water had pulled himself out, half entangled in slimy weeds like Jason coming out of the lake. He grabbed for some-thing in the boat... a big steel hook on a short wooden club.

"Your back!" yelled Bilal as the dude swung the hook, trying for bully boy's leg. Bully clumsily dodged, and the hook only ripped his jeans. Panting, he stumbled to join Bilal, then awkwardly spun to face the attack. The other big boy snatched an oar from the boat and, rearing back, readied to swing. The dude still down was moaning, his face in a puddle of melted ice cream, but the two other boys came on. The one with the hook snarled at Bilal, "Big mistake, whoever you are!"

Again, Bilal thought of the gun...

"That's enough!"

Annie appeared at the head of the dock, still in her apron, a dishrag in hand. "Michael! Bradley!" she roared, as if ordering all hands on deck in a storm. "Put that gear back in my boat right now or I'll take a rope's end to your asses!" She curled the dishrag suggestively.

Both big dudes seemed to suddenly morph into little boys caught boosting cookies. They returned their weapons to Annie's boat, laying them respectfully down. Annie studied the scene for a moment, Bully, nose bleeding, panting for breath. His jeans had tumbled around his knees but his belly kept him legal. Annie regarded the boy on the boards, his face like a mime's with blueberry zits, his hands clamped over his mistreated treasures, then she turned to Bilal.

"Sorry about your welcome to Rust, but this ain't the normal state of affairs." She frowned at panting Bully Boy. "You had some of that comin'!" She blew an exasperated sigh. "Why can't you just be nice, goddammit? Like you used to be. Somethin' else happen like this on my watch, an' you're eighty-sixed! You savvy?"

"Yeah, Annie," Bully Boy puffed, clumsily pulling up his jeans, the process rendered difficult by the torus of blubber around his waist.

Annie faced the two big dudes. "Same with you! Understand? You can all go to Ronald friggin' McDonalds down in Saunders Ferry!" She glanced at the scattered food on the dock, now being eyed by circling crows. "Try gettin' burgers like that from a clown!"

The bigger boys echoed Bully.

Annie glanced at the groaning dude. "Go home an' put some ice on 'em, Chris. Might keep 'em from turnin' blue. Michael, Bradley, take him home. ...An' hope I don't call your parents!"

"Okay, Annie," said one of the boys.

Bradley and Michael hoisted Chris, moaning and muttering onto his feet and helped him stumble away bent over like a question mark while clutching his zippered squirrel nuts. Annie wiped Bully Boy's nose with the dishrag. He resisted a moment but then gave in and let himself be medicoed.

"Ice will help with that, too," said Annie. She pinched Bully's nose, getting an ow! "Don't seem to be busted, but maybe it should be. ...You used to be such a *nice* boy, Quentin. What in hell's got into you?"

Quentin spit blood in the channel. "Got tired of bein' pushed around."

"I never seen any pushin'," said Annie. "Seems to me like *you* started pushin', an' damn if I can figure why."

Bilal's mouth had dropped open, hearing the fat boy's name. Now he scanned the dude again, looking for... he wasn't sure what. "Um?" he asked, "Quentin Tanner?" He couldn't see the fat boy's eyes, but felt a kind of pleading look from under the curly tumble of hair.

"...Yeah."

Annie was looking curious, and Bilal added quickly: "Somebody told me your name at school." He picked up Quentin's shirt and handed it to him.

"Thanks," said Quentin, slinging the shirt over a shoulder. "An' for the help. ...Want a ride to town?"

"...That would be cool," said Bilal, not knowing what else to say.

"Speakin' of help," said Annie. "Quentin, you clean up this mess! Crows can have the food, but I don't want ants in the ice cream. Next they'll be in the softee machine. There's a bucket, swab it down."

Quentin dropped to his hands and knees and started to gather the trampled feast. Bilal crouched beside him. "I'll do it, man, you get the bucket."

Annie untied her apron. "Stow the trash in this."

Bilal scooped paper cups and wrappings into Annie's apron, while Quentin dipped buckets of channel water and washed the goo off the dock.

"Just try an' be good again," growled Annie, as Quentin finished the job. "I don't wanna see no more bully crap, an' don't you think I haven't. What goes around always comes around... in case you ain't got that message today."

"Yeah, Annie. ...Sorry." Slinging his shirt again over a shoulder, Quentin walked away.

Annie smiled at Bilal as he gave her back the apron. "You did a good thing, my man, comin' to Quentin's rescue. Michael, Bradley an' Chris ain't 'bad'... seen 'em grow up since kindergarten. They wasn't out to kill nobody, though things got a little lively there after you came on deck. But Quentin's been pickin' on Bradley's brother... shakin' him down anyway." She glanced at Quentin's rolly back. "Don't know what's got into that boy. He's got a good heart, he just seems a little confused this year."

"I... guess it's that age," said Bilal, feeling a lot of confusion.

Annie smiled again. "You look like you know who you are." She slapped Bilal's back, almost knocking him over. "Next Tugboat Triple's on me. Quentin, too, if you take him in tow. Might be a good friend is all he needs to get him back on course."

"Looks like he's already got friends."

"Quentin's a hero to Jody. Stuck-up for Jody all his life. That's why I know he's got a good heart."

"You mean the... furry kid?" asked Bilal.

"Jody ain't had it easy. His mom was supposedly 'scared by a goat'... not that I believe that bilge. He's got some kind of genetic thing. I looked it up on the web. Harmless, but it makes him different, an' ignorant people hate anything different. He's a good kid but a little slow, an' smokin' weed ain't speeded him up. Don't know why he started that crap... far as I know Quentin don't. But, like I said, his life's been rough. His father swore nothin' like that could be his, an' run off a week after Jody was born. His mom couldn't look at him either, an' dumped him on a loony aunt. Offered to take him myself, but then his aunt wouldn't get welfare... not that she spends it on him."

"...Oh," said Bilal. "Guess you know everybody here."

Annie tossed a bun to a crow who was hovering like a helicopter. "Know a lot more than I want to sometimes. Rust ain't a bad little town like I said, but it's got its share of skeletons, an' all of 'em ain't in the graveyard. Shawn sorta lashed on to Quentin this summer. Kinda surprised me to see that, but maybe opposites do attract. Shawn used to be the school sports star. Raccoons almost won a few games when he played... 'least they didn't lose too bad. But he ain't on none of the teams this year, though I can't say I blame him since Swaggart was hired as coach... *that* son-of-a-bitch is a bully if I ever seen one. Shouldn't be workin' with kids at all, but I guess you get what you pay for, an' Skelly can't afford any better with all the school budget cuts. Swaggart claimed he could 'wipe out obesity' here, but all he does is torment kids who used to be happy bein' themselves... an' we still ain't won no games."

She flipped a fry to another crow. "Thought Shawn would be a good influence on Quentin. Shawn's always been a kind sorta kid, even if he don't gotta be with all them muscles an' movie-star looks. But they both started actin' like tough guys this summer. 'Course, boys their age need a man around to show 'em what bein' a man's all about. Otherwise they start playin' parts like they see in movies an' on TV, which ain't usually nothin' but overgrown boys."

"Or stupid monkeys," suggested Bilal.

Annie smiled. "I could tell you was smart the minute I seen you." She gave Bilal a thoughtful look. "By the way, where...?"

"I better go," Bilal said quickly. "...Sooo... Quentin can put some ice on his nose."

"You're welcome aboard my barge any time."

"Thanks... Um, bye." Bilal hurried away before Annie could ask where he was staying in town. He should have seen that coming; he wasn't being careful!

Quentin had righted his minibike and seemed to be checking for damage, though the thing was a wreck anyway. Then he mounted the battered machine, tied his shirt to the handlebars, and wrapped a rope on the engine's flywheel. After several puffing pulls the greasy engine sputtered to life, belching a cloud of oily blue smoke. Coming over after snagging his pack, Bilal saw a tarnished brass tag on the heavy mesh around it

TOTE GOTE

This place was full of visual jokes.

Quentin studied Devon's charm. "Um, can I...?"

"Sure," said Bilal, leaning close, and Quentin reached to hold it a moment.

"That's Anubis, the god of the dead."

"Not many people would know that."

"Maybe I ain't as dumb as I look."

"Or as bad as you act?"

Quentin scowled. "What's that s'posed to mean?"

Bilal shrugged. "Nothin'." He got on the back of the seat, his butt hanging off like elf boy's had, though Bilal had a lot more to bare, and put his arms around Quentin, his hands clasped under Quentin's boy-breasts, which felt like slippery melons of Jell-O.

Quentin looked over his shoulder, his eyes still hidden under his hair. "Um, *salaam.*"

"...Huh?" said Bilal.

"You don't understand *salaam?*"

"Duh!" snapped Bilal. "But I don't understand what's goin' on!"

Quentin flipped up the kickstand with the heel of a boot. "Wait till we get home."

THIRTEEN

Bilal was burning with questions, but trying to hold onto sweat-slicked Quentin and keep half his butt on the minibike's seat wasn't the time to be asking. They weren't going much over thirty, but the road was rough and full of holes and the Tote Gote's springs weren't very springy. The oily exhaust smoke watered his eyes, and the engine's clattering battered his ears. The loose chain nipped at his jeans cuffs, and the weathered pavement unrolling below would shred his skin if he fell. He jammed his chest to Quentin's back as if trying for a molecular bond and hugged the dude like a big squeeze toy.

It was less than a mile to town, but it seemed like several light-years on only impulse power. At last they rolled up to Gilman's Market and Quentin grounded the spark plug. The engine gave a final snort and graveyard silence settled. "Gotta get stuff for dinner."

Bilal hopped off the rusty machine as if he'd been riding a demon's back like in *The Exorcist II*. "I wanna know what's goin' on!"

"I said, wait till we get home."

"...Aight," said Bilal, though feeling pissed.

Quentin dropped the kickstand and got off the bike. "Can you pull up my jeans?"

Bilal yanked Quentin's jeans halfway up his dusky-mooned bottom.

"Thanks." Quentin puffed his way up the steps and paused at the top to look down at Bilal. "You can leave your pack, nobody'll steal it."

Bilal wiped Quentin's sweat from his eyes... blowback as they'd ridden. The town looked even deader than when he'd arrived on the bus; there were no vehicles at the cafe, which apparently only served breakfast and lunch, no people anywhere in sight, and the boarded windows of other buildings faced each other like blindfolded victims across the empty street. "'Cause there's nobody here, or 'cause you'd beat 'em up?"

"Whatever works for you."

Leaving his pack on the minibike's seat, Bilal followed Quentin into the store.

The place might really have been a saloon back in the days when people rode horses. Its lofty ceiling was lost in shadow, and a bar-like counter might once have served drinks, though now it was smothered with candy displays, disposable lighters and packaged snacks. Bare bulbs dangled from frayed-looking wires, but none were on and most of the light came through grimy front windows heavily plastered with SALE ads. A few beer signs lit the rear of the room, along with the glow of a glass-fronted cooler. Stuffed deer's heads stared down from the walls, their baleful eyes seeming to hate being dead and wishing the same on the living; but except for those and the old western look the place could have been a corner market anywhere in West Oakland.

There were the same uncertain shelves with painfully narrow aisles between, sagging with strange and off-brand things that wouldn't be found at Safeway. A lot of the cans were dented as if they were rejects from big-time stores, and some were missing labels, their contents printed with Magic Marker that didn't look convincing. The cereal shelf had Ruskets Flakes... whatever they were. A small display offered Halloween gear; cheap costumes that would probably burn, and masks that would probably melt on your face like in the *Halloween* movie. There were plastic skulls and skeletons, along with bags of nasty candy that only a homeless kid would eat. There was also a pile of pumpkins, many in strange or psychotic shapes as if they'd been grown in nuclear waste. A few rubber bats dangled on strings from what might have been an ancient gas light, and an equally ancient cash register, a greenish brass mechanical type, sat on one end of the bar. Lining the wall behind the bar were shelves with bottles of liquor and wine, chewing tobacco, and cigarettes.

"Did this used to be a saloon?" asked Bilal.

"Back in the gold-rush days," said Quentin, snagging a rusty shopping cart from a row of maybe a dozen. "An' a whorehouse, too."

"Huh?"

"A house inhabited by whores."

Quentin pushed the cart, squealing as if it was being kidnapped, between the ranks of rickety shelves, the floorboards creaking under his weight and his passage marked by a ripple effect of quaking cans and merchandise. Bilal looked around for the storekeeper, but no door buzzer or bell had rung and he didn't see the elderly man. He scanned for cameras but couldn't spot any.

"You drink beer?" asked Quentin, stopping at the cooler, his sweaty body gleaming in the blue fluorescent glow.

Bilal shrugged. "Who don't?"

Quentin put two sixers of Bud in the cart, then grabbed a quart of milk and sloppily started chugging it.

"Where's the store guy?" asked Bilal.

Quentin came up for air and burped. "Probably takin' a nap. You like mutton chops?"

"What are they?"

"Lamb chops with an attitude."

"Huh?"

"From grown-up sheep. The Indians raise 'em. Guess you could call it organic."

"I don't give a shit if somethin's organic as long as it doesn't taste like shit."

"That's a healthy attitude. How many can you eat?"

"How big are they?"

Quentin held up a big chunk of meat.

"One's enough for me," said Bilal. "I'm totally stuffed from Annie's. That tugboat triple was off the hook."

"I didn't get to eat much of mine."

Bilal gave Quentin Devon's smile. "I noticed." He went to the long wooden bar while Quentin continued shopping. Part of the counter was fronted with glass and there were guns inside, mostly cowboy revolvers, but also rifles and shotguns, along with bullets and shells. Bilal checked the ammunition; there was a box of 7.62 that might fit his Tokarev.

Of course he would throw it away. When he was sure he didn't need it.

Quentin clumped over with jingling chains like a fat outlaw kid from *Back To The Future*, and offered the milk to Bilal. "You like guns?"

Bilal took the half-empty carton and drank. "Depends on if they're aimed at me."

"I got one. A coach gun."

"That's cool," said Bilal, though he didn't know what a coach gun was. He pictured Swaggart with a cartoon cannon pointed at a fat kid.

Quentin rolled the complaining cart, containing a stack of mutton chops, a sack of potatoes, a dozen eggs, the sixers of beer and a gallon of milk, up to the ancient register. Then he went to the cigarette rack and took a blue pack of American Spirits. "You smoke?"

"No."

Quentin tossed the pack on the counter and stabbed a key on the register. A little bell rang, and a tab popped up in the window: NO SALE. The drawer snicked open, revealing money, though tired-looking and not very much.

Bilal cocked his head. "What you doin'?"

"What's it look like?" Quentin took a pencil and pad from the drawer.

"...Oh."

The sheepdog face regarded Bilal. "Think I was stealin' this stuff?"

"No."

"You didn't steal nothin', did you?"

"Fuck no!"

"Can you pull up my jeans again?"

"Can't you?"

Quentin patted the rolls of his middle. "Yeah, but they're hard to reach."

Bilal yanked up Quentin's jeans.

"Thanks." Quentin reached under the counter and pulled out a brown paper bag. "Do somethin' else useful."

Bilal began to bag the things while Quentin printed ponderously. Bilal recognized the childish style from the letter Jadd Taimur had gotten.

FOURTEEN

Back on the Gote from hell again, Bilal barely managed to stay on the seat while clutching the bulky grocery bag and trying to hang on to slippery Quentin. Thankfully the ride was short, back up the street to the rusty old bridge, where Quentin turned left on Channel Road. Beside the bridge tower was a small wooden house that looked like houses little kids drew; a simple square box with a high-peaked roof and a window with four panes of glass like a cross on either side of the door. Over the door was a rusty sign:

**HIGHWAY DEPARTMENT
BRIDGE 13**

The yard was a jungle of dead yellow weeds overgrowing the corpse of an ancient Ford pickup decomposing on four flat tires; and the house's backside jutted over the channel on rickety wooden pilings. Huge weeping willows spread over the roof, surrounding the house with an island of shade, and the air was almost comfortably cool. Bilal studied the bridge as they chugged to a stop. The traffic light was still glowing green. A rusty sign on the tower read

**NOTICE OF 14
DAYS REQUIRED**

and something else in smaller letters but too rusty to read.

"Required for what?" asked Bilal, getting gratefully off the bike as Quentin grounded the spark plug and the engine backfired once and died.

"To open the bridge," said Quentin. "When a boat wants to go through. They gotta send a letter fourteen days before, then they got a six hour window."

Bilal looked up at the bridge again, its iron as orange as the old minibike in the reddening rays of the lowering sun. Halfway up the tower was a rusty little control house of corrugated tin. "Somebody stays up there for six hours?"

"Usually me," said Quentin, kicking down the kickstand.

From down the road toward Annie's, the bell of Saint Toads clanked five times.

"So, now will you tell me...?" asked Bilal.

"Can you up pull up my jeans again?"

Bilal did it one-handed, holding the bag. "So...?"

"C'mon," said Quentin. He climbed a single sagging step to the rusty tin-roofed porch. Only a screen door guarded the house, and it didn't seem to be locked. Three other Tote Gotes stood on the porch, all missing parts like dissected cadavers.

The house smelled mostly of Quentin... boy-sweat, jeans, and old leather boots, oily hair and cigarette smoke. It had a Bates Motel kind of look, the furniture old enough to be old but not old enough to be worth anything. The small living room was filled by a couch, a coffee table, a brass floor lamp, and a small TV on a wooden stand. At least there was a cable box. The floor was bare boards where dust-bunnies ruled, and cobwebs clung in corners.

Behind the couch were three open doors, the middle one showing a long-legged stove of green and ivory porcelain and an ancient refrigerator with its motor on top. The right-hand door showed a little bedroom with a brass-framed double bed, while the door on the left revealed a bathroom inhabited by a high-tank toilet.

"Put the stuff in the kitchen," said Quentin, then jingled into the bathroom and didn't close the door.

Water-sound echoed loudly in the ghost town silence as Bilal took the groceries into the kitchen and put them on a wooden table.

Beside the fridge was a doorway filled with a rippling greenish glow. Three steps led down to an enclosed porch that jutted over the channel. This was obviously Quentin's den, if only judged by how it smelled. Three walls had windows, screened and open, that let in the shimmering emerald light. To the left was an ancient dresser and a messy iron-framed single bed where tigers might have tangled. The sheets were slick with body oil and grimy gray as rats. There was also a strong scent of something that Jody had blatantly emanated and Bilal hadn't done since Devon's death.

Respecting Quentin's space, Bilal remained on the second step while scanning the green-lit room. The nearest wall, the back of the house, was plastered with pictures of Tote Gotes... there was an elderly Mac and a printer atop a battered desk. There was also a photo of elf boy Shawn, shirtless and scarfing a burger at Annie's; and several of a younger Jody, even then a little furry -- at least for a kid of his age -- and chubby in a lazy way, though he seemed to have gained his huge belly this summer, probably under the influence of weed. The floor was littered with dirty socks, candy bar wrappers, potato chip bags, cookie boxes and cigarette packs. As Bilal had already noticed, Quen-tin didn't seem to wear shorts.

On a homemade shelf was an old stereo and a stack of classic rock CDs: The Rolling Stones, Creedence Clearwater, Boston, Journey and REO. Another shelf held a row of books, and that surprised Bilal... Quentin didn't look like a reader. Among the titles were *Lord Of The Rings, Watership Down, The Jungle Book, Kim, The Catcher In The Rye, Huckleberry Finn* and *The Wind In The Willows*. Under the bed was a big tool box. On a packing crate beside the bed was a table lamp without a shade, a tuna can brimming with cigarette butts, and a new-looking paperback book. It was one of those books like "Macs For Morons." Its title was *Islam For Idiots*.

In contrast to the male teen mess, the room's right-hand corner looked recently cleaned, and there was a narrow, iron-framed cot almost neatly made.

"That's your bed, man. Cool?" said Quentin, jingling up behind Bilal. "Got it at Whatley's Second-Hand. I gassed the mattress to kill any cooties, but there probably wasn't none."

"Yeah, it's cool. ...Sorry for snoopin'."

"It's your room, too." Then Quentin actually smiled. "Cousin."

"How do you gas a mattress?"

"Wrap it up in plastic, then fill it with gas from the stove with a hose."

"Guess that would kill any cooties."

"Then I aired it in the sun so there ain't no smell." Quentin hesitated. "Guess you coulda slept with me, but I figured you wouldn't wanna."

"Why not, you got cooties?"

Quentin shrugged. "I take up a lotta room."

Bilal laughed and made the obvious gesture.

Quentin looked relieved. "Yeah, that too. ...I got a dresser for your clothes, but it don't come apart like the bed so I couldn't bring it on the Gote. We can use Mr. Whatley's truck, but I gotta fix it first."

"Thanks," said Bilal. "Jadd... grandpa... is supposed send my stuff next week. I have a lot of books."

"We can find a shelf at Whatley's. He's got a lot of junk like that since people been leavin' town."

Bilal went to the cot and took off his pack. "Now...?"

An old-fashioned telephone rang, mounted on the kitchen wall, and Quentin grabbed the receiver. "Bridge thirteen. ...Hey. ...I'm cool. ...Sure, but..." He glanced at Bilal. "Wait till dinnertime, okay?"

Bilal climbed the steps to the kitchen as Quentin hung up the phone. "Jody?" he asked.

"How did you know?"

"A friend would check on how you were after what happened at Annie's."

Quentin considered that and nodded. "He always hangs with me after school an' usually has dinner. His aunt don't cook worth shit... says 'food is a sin if it tastes good' an' does her best to make sure it don't. Shawn's probably grounded an' can't use his phone."

"So, now...?"

"Wait." Quentin put the milk and eggs in the fridge, then ripped two cans of Bud from a sixer and handed one to Bilal.

"Thanks." Bilal popped the tab and took a gulp, suddenly realized he was thirsty and sucked down several swallows. He burped and wiped his mouth, then said, "But, you're white."

Quentin popped the other can. "That's what everybody thinks. But you probably don't understand."

"I don't," said Bilal. "My uncle *was* your dad, wasn't he?"

"C'mon." Quentin descended the steps to his room and opened a door overlooking the channel. Rickety stairs led down to a dock about the size of Annie's. The dock was almost under the bridge, beside the tower's concrete base, half hidden by reeds and the huge willow trees. Its boards were covered with soft green moss, and tied to a post was an old wooden boat, twelve feet long with an outboard motor and painted faded orange. Its sides were stenciled, **BRIDGE 13**.

Quentin led the way down to the dock, the steps vocalizing under his weight and sagging somewhat ominously. "Um, this might be a cool place to pray. ...Like in private, y'know? East is that way, across the channel."

It was a cool place, thought Bilal, sort of peaceful and secret, like something in a story where kids could be alone and dream. But he frowned. "I don't pray."

Quentin looked surprised. "Thought you were a Muslim?"

"I said I don't pray!" Bilal stepped to Quentin, belly to belly, and jammed a finger to Quentin's chest. "What the hell is goin' on? If you're my cousin why aren't you black? An' where's your brother?"

"Sacramento," said Quentin, standing unmoved against Bilal. "He goes to college there."

"Is he white, too?"

"Mom was white," said Quentin.

Bilal stepped back a pace. "...Oh."

"Wanna sit down an' talk?" Without waiting for an answer, Quentin plopped down on the edge of the dock, his boots swinging over the water. Bilal sat down beside him. Quentin took a gulp of beer, and a few seconds later Bilal did, too. Both boys burped. Quentin dug in a pocket and pulled out his cigarette pack. "So, you don't smoke?"

"No."

"'Cause it's forbidden?"

"It's not forbidden, I just don't."

"'Cause it ain't healthy?"

"More like expensive."

Quentin tapped Bilal's beer can. "But drinkin' is forbidden."

"Lots of things are forbidden if you believe they're what God said instead of just advice from people. An' a lot of it's way out of date. ...Like, pork used to be full of worms so it wasn't safe to eat. An' if Christians believed everything in their Bible they'd still kill people for workin' on Sunday. Or burn animals to 'please the Lord.' Or make other people slaves... 'slaves, obey your earthly masters with deep respect and fear.' Jesus supposedly said that."

"You read the Bible?"

Bilal took another swallow of beer. "It's only a book that people wrote, tryin' to say they understood God. It ain't much different from the Quran unless you want it to be."

"I was tryin' to respect you," said Quentin. "I mean, what you believed."

"...Thanks," said Bilal. "I saw the book. Maybe I should read it, too, 'cause I feel like an idiot most of the time."

"You mean about God?" asked Quentin. "Like, whether you should pray or not?"

Bilal drank more beer. "Prayin' feels like beggin', an' maybe I begged too much."

"I feel you, man," said Quentin.

Bilal made a face. "Don't try an' talk black."

"'Cause it's uncool?"

"No, 'cause it sounds retarded, even when black people do it."

"A lot of white kids do it."

"Which sounds more retarded."

"What about nigger with an A?"

"What about retard with an A?"

"Don't call Jody a retard, okay?"

"I won't unless he calls me one."

"Think I could beat you up?"

"Maybe. Is that important?"

"No." Quentin fired a cigarette with a disposable lighter and blew out a rippling ghost of smoke that drifted up toward the bridge. Bilal watched the ghost fade away, then said, "I know this much: my dad had a brother... your dad. An' he got killed on that bridge. ...Um, sorry about his head."

Quentin looked down at the tree-shadowed water. "Nobody ever found it."

"Sorry," said Bilal again.

"I used to go divin' here, lookin' for it. I wanted to put it in the coffin. Like, that would be the right thing to do."

"Guess it would," agreed Bilal. "But, you'd have to dig up the grave. Wouldn't you be scared?"

"Why would I be scared of my dad, even if he's a skeleton now? I wanted his bones to rest in peace. All together, y'know?" Quentin scowled. "There's a story about his ghost hauntin' the bridge on foggy nights."

"Guess there would be," said Bilal, looking up at the iron skeleton. "So... he married a white lady?"

Quentin exhaled another ghost. "She got killed when I was three. Up in Sacramento. Some bangers was shootin' at each other an' she got caught in the middle."

"Sorry, man."

Quentin shrugged. "I never really knew her. ...How much do you know when you're three? Dad got this job on the bridge to get us out of the city. My brother, Darien, was eight then. People thought we were adopted."

Bilal scanned Quentin carefully, remembering how, back at Annie's, he'd been searching for something but wasn't sure what. He noted the slightly dusky skin that could have passed for dirty, the small-bridged shape of the snubby nose... it would have looked wider if Quentin's cheeks hadn't been so chubby. Before he could think it might not be cool, he reached out and pushed back Quentin's hair, revealing eyes that seemed to change color, from brown to green to almost blue depending upon the light; and here were the greens of the water and leaves, the rust and browns of the branches and bridge, and the deepening blue of the evening sky.

Bilal smiled. "Yo, cousin."

"Yo, cousin," said Quentin, smiling back. "Anyway, since everybody thought we were white, it made things easier around here."

"But, Annie said everyone liked your dad."

"They did," said Quentin. "After they got to know him. Like, as a person instead of a color. But not at first. Except Mr. Gilman."

Bilal nodded. "I met him when I got off the bus. He told me a black man saved his life in World War Two."

"Mr. Gilman was hero. Got a bunch of medals. People here respect stuff like that. So, when he treated my dad with respect, other people did, too."

"But you never told anybody? ...That you weren't adopted?"

Quentin drank more beer. "By then we were accepted."

Bilal sipped beer and considered. "Guess I can understand that. It would be like sayin' you're gay... like, comin' out. People would have to accept you again for bein' somethin' different... or not what they always thought you were. An' maybe some of them wouldn't."

Quentin scowled. "That's exactly what it would be! ...Or comin' out you're a Muslim."

Bilal smiled. "Which might be harder to accept. That's probably why your name is Tanner instead of Taimur."

"Never thought about it."

"No reason you would," said Bilal. "Do Shawn an' Jody know?"

"Jody always knew, ever since we were little. I told Shawn this summer." Quentin touched Bilal's shoulder. "I knew I had a cousin somewhere. Dad talked about his family sometimes."

"It's your family, too," said Bilal. "But there's only me an' Jadd Taimur."

"Still good to know I got family."

Bilal thought for a moment. "You must have told Jody an' Shawn I was comin'... they'd wonder why you bought the bed... but you didn't say I was black."

"How do you know?"

"'Cause they would have figured I was your cousin, seein' me at Annie's. They weren't expecting me to be black. An' you kept it on the under. I could tell you were scopin' me out, but I thought you were checkin' my flex."

"I didn't know you'd be *this* black. I thought you might look... I dunno... Arabian, I guess. Like Aladdin in the movie. Dad was pretty light."

"My mom was dark," said Bilal. "Guess I took after her."

"An' half the school was there," said Quentin. "I needed time to think."

"Are people around here racist?"

"I wouldn't call 'em that. Not after they get to know somebody. ...For sure, there's all the usual jokes..."

"Like blanket-asses for Indians?"

"Yeah, but they ain't really mean. They call themselves that sometimes. Don't you call yourself a nigga?"

"No, 'cause it sounds retarded. An' Swaggart sounded mean when he yelled blanket-asses an' fat-hater shit."

Quentin drank beer and burped. "Swaggart is a retard. But he mostly hates fat kids an' gays. Says they're a threat to America. ...But, there's no gay kids around here so he has to hate on fat ones. Skelly hired him 'cause he said he'd make all the kids healthy winners."

Bilal smiled. "I thought it was cool to be a loser."

"Only if you're retarded."

"I never thought you'd look white," said Bilal. "You should have wrote you had a computer, we could have traded pics."

"I didn't think about that. But I sent you a pic... I wrote another letter."

Bilal tensed. "When did you send it?"

"Gave it to Jody to mail on Tuesday, but he lost it somewhere. He always forgets things an' loses stuff. He's done it all his life."

"...Oh," said Bilal. "Then it didn't get sent?"

"No. Why?"

"It's not important."

Quentin chugged the rest of his beer and threw the can in the water. He saw Bilal's look and smiled. "Salamanders live in 'em. The tree-huggers built 'em habitats, but they like cans a lot better. There's more of 'em livin' around this bridge than anywhere else in the channel."

"Oh."

"So, you don't believe in holy stuff?"

"...I'm not sure anymore." Bilal looked up at the sky through the willow leaves and the bridge's bones. "Sometimes I feel like I'm bein' tested." He took another gulp of beer. "But I ain't gonna blow your cover if that's what you're worried about."

Quentin scowled again. "What's that s'posed to mean?"

"Like wearin' a kufi or prayin' at school."

"That's your cover, not mine."

Bilal smiled."What's your cover?"

"What's that s'posed to mean?"

"Nothin'." Bilal drank the rest of his beer and tossed the can in the water. "But, what about me livin' here?" He patted his chest. "Bein' this black."

"You're my cousin, man. That's all anybody needs to know." Quentin flipped his cigarette into the water. "So, what's your story, Bilal? An' I know it's more than it said in the letter. Somebody's after your ass, huh? Gang shit in the 'hood? Like what killed my mom?"

"...Yeah," said Bilal. "But it's stupid monkey-boys playin' retarded monkey games... except people die on the real."

The bell of Saint Toads clanked six times. The sky had darkened to gunmetal dusk, and a movie graveyard kind of mist was beginning to rise from the water.

"Tell me about it later," said Quentin. "Gotta start makin' us dinner." He thought for a moment. "'If you remain good and strong of heart, even if the enemy should rush here, your Lord will help you.'"

Bilal cocked his head. "You get that from *Islam For Idiots?*"

"No, the Quran. The one that belonged to my dad."

Bilal smiled. "There's a lot of you on the under."

"What's that s'posed to mean?"

"You're not as dumb as you look."

"...Well, like I said, I got a gun, even if your Lord don't help you."

Bilal looked up at the sky again. "Maybe nobody's Lord is helpin' no more 'cause too many people believe in guns."

FIFTEEN

A bike rattled into the weedy front yard as Bilal followed Quentin back up to the kitchen. A moment later the screen door banged and Jody shambled in, still minus his 'beater and shiny with sweat, his jeans cuffs dragging over his sneaks; and Bilal found himself amazed again how furry and goat-like he was. The kid was just so awesomely ugly he was actually oxymoronically cute. His reek of dirty boy and dope, like a stoner kid from the Pet Sematary, flooded the air with funkiness, and the seminal scent was stronger as if he'd just had a session. Like a lot of "slow kids" he didn't try to hold back his belly and looked like he was following it, his shoulders slumped and his arms dangling down. If, as Quentin had said, his aunt only fed him nasty food, he must have dined with Quentin a lot, and maybe also at Annie's. Jody's narrow yellow eyes, still reddened a little from weed, widened when he saw Bilal.

"This is my cousin," said Quentin, pulling the string on a bare light bulb as dusk slowly settled outside. "Remember I told you he was comin'?"

Jody's voice was a squeaky bleat. "Yeah, but he sure black!"

"Don't say that!" growled Quentin.

Bilal smiled. "Why not? I am. Just don't call me a nigga."

"Okay." Jody offered a furry paw, not even close to being clean and showing all-too obvious signs of what was suggested by his smell. "Hi, I'm Jody."

"Bilal," said Bilal, shaking hands with the kid, and resisting afterward the urge to wash his own in the sink.

"I'm a little retarded," said Jody, "just so ya don't expect a lot."

"Don't call yourself that!" snapped Quentin.

"Why not? I am."

"So am I sometimes," said Bilal.

Jody giggled, displaying his bottle-opener teeth, which he obviously didn't brush. "You just say dat ta be nice. But it's nice." It was hard to tell if he was stoned or really just retarded. "Can I have a beer?" he asked.

Quentin handed him a Bud. The kid popped the can, drank and burped, then wiped what passed for a fuzzy chin. "Can I gets a punkin' tamorrow? Make a jacky lantern an' put it on your porch?"

"Sure," said Quentin. "But you should put it on your own porch."

"Can't. My aunt say Halloween is Satan's celebration of sin."

"Your aunt's full of shit," muttered Quentin. He twisted a knob on the spider-legged stove and fired the broiler with his lighter.

Jody turned to Bilal. "She call me Satan's bastard when she get da spirit."

"The spirit of what?" asked Bilal.

"Da Lord Jesus Christ, her personal savior."

"Sounds like she is full of shit," said Bilal.

"She used ta burn me with cigarettes 'cause Jesus give her revalations. I was sent from hell ta test her faith so I gotta be resisted."

"Way more than shit," said Bilal.

"Fluently," said Jody.

Quentin unwrapped the meat. "Jody, set the table."

Jody went to a cupboard. "Mutt chops, cool! I can eat three."

"I know," said Quentin, then turned to Bilal. "Sure you don't want more than one?"

"Guess I'll have two," said Bilal.

Jody pointed to a farm supply calendar tacked to the wall above the sink. "S'posed ta does a test today."

"Oh yeah, I forgot," said Quentin. "We better do it now."

"Goody!" cried Jody and clapped his paws.

"Don't say that, it sounds retarded."

"Sorry."

Bilal asked, "A test for school?"

"Nah. Bridge test," said Quentin. "Gotta open it once a month to see if it still works. Wanna come with us?"

"Sure."

The mist was growing thicker as Bilal and Jody followed Quentin out to the base of the tower. Then, Quentin leading, Bilal coming last, they climbed a ladder to the control house, emerging onto a platform thirty feet above the road. A green glow came from the traffic light below the iron grating.

Bilal went to the rail and scanned around. The mist was slowly invading the town like evil fog in a Stephen King movie. Most of the houses and buildings were dark, and many street lamps weren't working. Those that did were ancient types with dimly burning bulbs. The Ideal Lunch was closed, though Flying Horse Gas and the market were open; and Mr. Gilman was out on his porch stacking psychotic pumpkins. Distant lights of what might have been farms were slowly being snuffed by the fog. The spire of Saint Toads loomed out of the mist like a drowning finger pointing to heaven; and farther away up Channel Road was the glow of the Burger Barge sign. A few headlights of cars and trucks wormed their way down narrow roads through a nighted patchwork of farmland fields. A semi-truck loaded with hay bales rumbled through town and beneath Bilal's feet, its tires whining over the bridge deck. The church bell clanked seven times; and he wondered what Jadd was doing... probably praying, maybe for him.

"Thinkin' about what you left?" asked Quentin, coming to stand beside Bilal.

"How did you know?"

Jody joined them at the rail. "'Cause when da sun go down you gets a little sad sometimes."

Bilal touched Devon's charm and nodded. "My grandfather said it's a time when young men get lonely an' try to find comfort beyond earthy things."

"Happens ta me a lot," said Jody. "An' I'm only a kid."

Quentin opened the control house door and switched on a light inside. Old-fashioned windows of little square panes cast a golden glow in the mist. Inside was massive machinery like the rusty, cob-webbed lockdown gears in the remake of *House On Haunted Hill*. There were mammoth cables, long iron levers, and a Dumpster-sized electric motor. An amber light burned on a spider-webbed panel where two dusty gauges showed VOLTAGE, their needles reading 440. Another pilot light was green. There were huge copper switches like Igor threw when his master was making a monster. There was also a low but powerful hum like a transformer on a telephone pole. In a corner was a little desk and a wooden swivel chair. On the desk was a big black book like Lovecraft's *Necronomicon*.

"Can I does it?" asked Jody.

"Sure." Quentin plopped down in the chair.

Grinning like a stoned little kid -- or Igor making a monster -- Jody threw one of the big copper switches. Though the grimy windows, Bilal saw the traffic lights change to red on both sides of the bridge. Jody threw another switch, almost dancing with goatish glee as warn-ing bells began to clang. Bilal went to the door and looked down through the grating: as he'd thought when he'd first seen the bridge, a wooden arm was lowering across the road below. A dusty pickup rolling through town, slowed and came to a squealy stop.

Jody grasped one of the long iron levers, which seemed to take all his strength to pull. The low hum changed to a vibrating whine like a jet plane getting ready for takeoff. Blue sparks flickered inside the huge motor, which shook the floor as it powered up and rattled the tin-sheeted walls. The overhead light dimmed to orange. Mammoth gears began to turn, creaking, squealing, rumbling, and breaking nets of spiderwebs. Rust flakes popped from tightening cables. The whole bridge started to tremble like a huge iron monster coming to life. There were agonized groans and metallic screams, and a ponderous, rhythmic clank. Bilal pressed his nose to a window as the bridge's massive center section slowly began to rise.

"All da way?" bleated Jody above the shrieks of straining steel.

Quentin opened the big black book and pulled a pencil from the desk. "Yeah, but don't slam it, the cables are old."

Jody looked scary, dancing around in the flickering blue electric glare from the keening motor. The scent of ozone filled the air, along with the smell of hot copper. The squealing and groaning, the clatter and clanking, seemed to go on for an hour, though it was probably less than five minutes before Jody shoved back the lever and struggled to pull another. All the sounds suddenly ceased except the clang of the warning bells. The bridge's center section hung forty feet above the channel. A car had joined the pickup waiting on the road below, and headlights glowed on the opposite shore as another vehicle came to a stop.

Quentin wrote something in the book. "Okay, bring it down."

Jody attacked the levers again, pushing one, pulling another, but the racket and tremoring wasn't as much as the center section slowly descended.

Suddenly there was a massive CLUNK, shaking the whole rusty structure again, and everything clashed to a stop.

"Shit!" muttered Quentin. Rising, he grabbed a long iron bar and squirmed around the smoking motor into the mass of motionless gears.

"What's wrong?" asked Bilal.

Quentin levered the bar into something. "Pawl jammed again."

"Paul?" asked Bilal.

"Pawwwl," said Jody. "Da thing dat go clank."

Quentin looked caught in some gigantic clock as he struggled and strained on the bar. Specters of mist drifted up around him through an opening where the cables went through.

"Need any help?" asked Bilal.

"No, an' stay away... but thanks." Muscles buried deep in fat now stood out in Quentin's arms as he threw all his weight on the bar.

Bilal turned to Jody and whispered, "Is this how it happened?"

"Mean his dad gettin' croaked?"

"Yeah."

"Yeah, he gots his head chopped off doin' what Quentin doin'." Jody made the throat-slicing gesture. "Abundantly."

Something clanked and Quentin jerked back. The gears released with a grinding screech and started turning again. The massive cables quivered and thrummed like a gargantuan bass guitar. Jody leaned close to Bilal and whispered, "His ghost come back ta look for it on foggy nights like dis."

"What?" puffed Quentin, worming his way out of the gears as

they squealed and rumbled around him.

"Nothin'," said Jody.

The bridge finally closed with another huge CLUNK that might have shaken the town. The overhead bulb brightened again as the smoking motor creaked to a stop. Jody switched off the warning bells and the wooden arms began to rise. He threw another switch and the traffic lights went green. The vehicles drove across the bridge and vanished in the mist.

"Can I smoke?" asked Jody, as Quentin, now greasy and streaked with rust, squeezed around the enormous motor.

"Yours or mine?" asked Quentin.

"Yours, I'm out."

"Good." Quentin pulled out his American Spirits. "I wish you'd stop smokin' that shit."

Jody shrugged. "Makes me feel like I ain't so bad."

"No, it makes you retarded."

"But I already am."

"Not that much."

"Sufficiently."

"Um," said Bilal as Jody took a cigarette. "Why should you feel bad?"

"'Cause I'm ugly an' retarded."

"Don't say that!" snapped Quentin.

"Sorry."

"...Well," said Bilal, not sure what he meant. "Maybe you're just bein' tested."

"Huh?"

"...Kinda like this bridge."

"...Mean, by God? Like, ta see if I work right?"

"Yeah, like that."

"Yeah," agreed Quentin. "Satan don't want you to work right."

Jody giggled. "Yeah, he'd want me ta work wrong."

SIXTEEN

The bell of Saint Toads clanked ten times, muffled by the smothering mist like the ghostly bell of a sunken ship. Quentin, naked except for his rings, plopped his wobbly bulk on his bed. "Guess you had a long day."

Bilal stripped off his sweaty boxers, sat down on his cot and yawned. "It was kinda long. Like Frodo startin' out on his quest with the Black Riders after his ass."

"Or a spy movie," said Quentin. "Getting' shot at by gangsters, an' doin' that James Bond trick on the train to throw 'em off your trail." He smiled and added, "Mine's like that, too."

"Huh?" said Bilal, yawning again.

Quentin got to his feet and gathered two handfuls of belly blubber, revealing the tip of a rather plump shaft protruding from a puff of chub. "Maybe 'cause we're cousins."

Bilal laughed. "Or just fat. An' I got most of mine this summer."

Quentin sat back down. "Makes it kinda hard to... you know?"

Bilal held up a thumb and two fingers. But then he frowned. "I haven't done it for awhile."

"How come?" asked Quentin.

"Too much stuff on my mind." Bilal got under the blankets, noting they'd been recently washed -- at least compared to Quentin's

-- then pillowed his head on his arms and sighed. "I *wish* it was a movie, startin' from that day in the park when Devon smiled at the monkeys. Maybe we coulda left before the shitty ending."

"Sorry about your friend, Bilal."

"Yeah, me too."

"Don't worry." Leaning over the mass of his middle, Quentin pulled something from under the bed.

"That's a coach gun?" asked Bilal, eyeing a short, double-barreled shotgun.

"Ten-gauge," said Quentin. "Like they used to blow away bandits tryin' to rob the stages."

"What do you use it for?"

"Mostly shootin' rats at the dump 'cause they spread diseases. The deputy sheriff pays me a bounty, fifty cents apiece. ...Did you have a gun in the 'hood?"

Jody had left around nine, a little buzzed from three cans of beer, one with their mutton-chop dinner, which had also included mashed potatoes, corn-on-the-cob and vanilla ice cream, and two while watch-ing *Nightmare On Elm Street*... there was a Halloween marathon. He'd been weaving a bit on his bike as he'd pedaled away in the fog.

Bilal and Quentin had finished the beer down on the dock in the mist, which glowed bloody red from a light on the bridge, a warning to boats it was closed. Bilal had told Quentin everything... except about having the gun. After all, he would throw it away. Maybe to-morrow in the channel.

"Most kids don't have guns," Bilal said now. "Only most of the monkeys."

"Well," said Quentin. "I don't see how they could find you here, but I got your back if they do."

"This shit is for real, you know, not a movie."

Quentin got up and opened the door. Aiming the shotgun into the night, he cocked a hammer and fired. The heavy gun bucked against his shoulder. The blast could have woken the dead. "That real enough for you?"

The telephone rang in the kitchen, and Quentin, toting the smoking gun, went up to answer it. "Bridge thirteen. ...Hey, man. ...Yeah, I figured that. ...I'm cool. Got punched a few times is all. My cousin got here." He smiled at Bilal. "Yeah, he rocks. ...Tomorrow? I gotta fix Mr. Whatley's truck, but we can go fishin' later. Meet you at the Barge for lunch. ...Okay, man. ...I... yeah, you too."

"Shawn?" asked Bilal, as Quentin padded back to his bed.

"His brother blamed *him* for startin' the fight, so he got grounded in his room. He just snuck out to call me when his parents went to bed."

"A good friend would."

Quentin had found an apple crate for Bilal to use as a bedside table, and Bilal had unpacked "Aladdin's lamp" and set it on the box. He'd put the Quran beside it -- just a habit, he supposed -- along with Akeem's Bible. "So, what's his brother got against you?"

It was hard to read a face with no eyes, and Quentin's were hidden under his hair, but he might have looked uneasy. "It's mostly his mom an' dad. They think I'm the reason he dropped out of sports."

"Are you?"

"He just got tired of stupid games an'... pretendin' to be what he wasn't."

"Like Swaggart's idea of a 'winner?'"

"That's a good way to say it. Swaggart told Shawn's parents that bein' fat was like a disease an' Shawn would catch it from me."

"That's retarded."

"If you did a Google for retarded there'd be Swaggart's picture. Assholes like *him* are like a disease 'cause they make other people catch hate. An' that's killed more people than any disease."

"You really ain't as dumb as you look."

"Maybe it's my cover." Quentin slipped a new shell into the gun and slid it back under the bed. "You like fishin'?"

"Never did it."

"It's easy, the fish do most of the work." Quentin got under his blankets, the bed springs creaking loudly, then switched off his lamp. "So, you don't pray, even at night?"

Bilal gazed up at the rusty tin roof in the dim red glow of the bridge warning light beyond the misted windows. "Sometimes in my mind I still do… kinda like whether I want to or not… but I'm not sure who I'm talkin' to. …Do you?"

"Sometimes in my mind, an' kinda like whether I want to or not."

*   *   *

Bilal didn't know what awakened him… maybe the call of the lonely church bell. The red-tinted mist still shrouded the windows, droplets running like blood down the glass, and the night was death-ly silent. He could hear Quentin's breathing slow and deep. The smell of Quentin ruled the room… and yet he scented Devon!

But he'd taken the MacBook out of his pack to show Devon's pictures to Quentin, and lain Devon's jacket on the foot of the cot. Yet the scent also seemed to be on his pillow like all those nights when Devon slept-over; and just as he'd awakened – maybe just for a second – he'd thought he'd felt Devon's rolly warmth nestled comfortingly beside him. Then, not knowing why, he slipped from the bed and opened the door overlooking the channel.

Dimly seen through the drifting mist, the boat gently nuzzled the dock below as the ghost of a breeze rippled the willows and whis-pered through their branches. Bilal gazed up at the bridge tower, its top receding into the fog like a huge rusty ladder to heaven. The warning lamp shone like a watchful red eye, and there was a fainter greenish glow from the traffic light over the road. Quietly closing the door behind him, Bilal descended the steps. The moss on the dock was soft underfoot and gave off a faint spicy scent. He studied the boat for a moment – he'd never been in a boat before -- then eased himself in and sat on a seat.

"We was gonna go fishin' someday, remember?"

Bilal stared up at the bridge. A figure sat on the concrete base ten feet above the dock… a rolly-fat shirtless boy in jeans, his sneaks swinging over the water. He looked like he had on that hot afternoon before the monkeys murdered him.

"'Course I remember," said Bilal. "…Yo, I'm dreamin', right?"

Devon smiled his Devon smile. "If you're a dreamer dreamin' a dream don't axe your dream if you're dreamin'."

Bilal moved to get out of the boat, to cross the dock and be closer to Devon.

"Careful, man, or you'll fall in."

Bilal almost did, one foot on the dock and one in the boat, but made it out and gazed up at Devon. "Did you make it, man? To... somewhere good?"

"Oh sure; I'm one of the seventy-two virgins."

"...*What?*"

"Where does it say they'll all be girls?" Devon smiled again. "Allah has a sense of humor. A lot of the Faithful forget that."

"On whose name be praise. ...Um, is my grandfather okay?"

"Yo, Bilal, I'm not a Jinn, so don't rub your lamp an' axe for wishes." Devon grinned. "But it's cool if you wanna rub somethin' else."

"...I ain't felt like it," said Bilal.

"'Cause I got killed?"

"That kinda takes me out of the mood."

Devon made the obvious gesture. "Wanna make this dream a wet one?"

"I'm still not in the mood."

"Denying yourself good things on earth don't score no points with God. It's like throwin' away a present He gave you."

Bilal frowned. "You barely got to open yours."

"It's not about how long you live, but what you *do* with your life that counts. We're here for a good time, not for a long time. Some people could live a hundred years an' never do nothin' worth shit, or make God happy by bein' happy an' makin' other people happy." Devon patted his pillow of belly. "Souls ain't judged by BMI or how much you denied yourself. An' losin' one *really* makes you a loser."

Bilal had to remind himself that Devon weighed less than nothing now. ...Unless a soul could be weighed.

"Souls *are* weighed," said Devon. "The good you done against the bad, an' how much you loved against how much you hated."

"Can you read my mind?" asked Bilal.

"Nah, I just know how you think."

"Your soul must weigh a ton of good."

"Ain't been on a scale yet. Most of people's suffering is caused by other people. If you make yourself suffer you're bein' a fool."

"Tell that to Jody, he's suffered all his life."

"An' why...?"

"'Cause people... Oh." said Bilal.

Devon shaded his eyes with a hand like an Indian boy scanning the mist. "Why are some people starvin' to death? Why are some people so poor? Why are some people dyin' 'cause they can't get help or medicine?"

"I get it," said Bilal.

Devon smiled again. "You better go back to bed. You had a long day, gettin' shot at by wanksters an' doin' that James Bond trick on the train. ...An' all that walkin'. Wanna see me fade away? Cool FX."

"Wait!" cried Bilal. "Assuming this ain't a dream, why did you take so long to come back?"

Devon cocked his head. "'Assuming?' Ain't that soundin' white?"

"Or just not soundin' stupid."

"You wanted me to follow you. You even prayed I would, even if you didn't know it."

"But, you could have come back a long time ago."

Devon seemed to shiver. "Too many ghosts in the 'hood. Like you said to Akeem about skeletons, 'cept nobody hauls 'em away."

"Don't tell me you're scared of ghosts."

"Some of 'em are are pretty scary. Like crazy people who wander the streets all alone inside themselves."

"Can't they go to the light?"

"They never believed there was a light. The light's always there, but they can't see it."

"Why can't they see it?"

"'Cause they never look for it."

*   *   *

The lonely church bell clanked five times. Bilal opened his eyes to the dim red light. Mist still shrouded the windows, and Devon's jacket was pressed to his cheek, cuddled like a teddy bear. Had it only been a dream? ...But there were bits of moss on his feet. Then he heard a soft creaking of bed springs to an obvious rhythm and wondered who Quentin was dreaming about.

SEVENTEEN

Bilal stood under the rushing shower in a rusty claw-footed tub. Steam engulfed the little bathroom like warm white fog in a new universe where nothing had been created yet. Bilal was lost in his own creation, ecstatically plying two fingers and thumb; and maybe because it had been so long the Big Bang left him breathless. Panting, he slumped against the wall and let the water pour over him. Then a shadow materialized beyond the plastic curtain. The curtain flew back and there was a knife!

"Eee, eee, eee, eee!"

Bilal dodged away and slipped, plopping down on his butt in the tub. "Damn, man!" he yelled as Jody burst into laughter. "The hell you do that for?"

Jody grinned like an evil faun clutching a wicked butcher knife. He only wore his jeans and sneaks as if he'd slept in them. "Quentin say you like scary movies."

"I like to watch 'em, not star in 'em!"

Jody's yellow eyes went sly. "I knows what you was doin'."

Bilal got up and shut off the shower. "Yeah? Don't you?"

"All da time. Some days I can't stop. My aunt say I goin' to hell for castin' my seed upon da ground."

"I thought that's where you came from."

Jody laughed. "Dat's a good one."

Bilal recalled what he'd heard about goats... weren't they known for being horny? At least boy goats.

Jody puffed his chest. "I knows ten different ways!"

"...Cool," said Bilal, who only knew seven -- and Devon had taught him four of those -- though his recent weight gain had reduced his options.

Jody seemed to have warmed to the subject, judging by the bulge in his jeans, which was impressive for his age; and Bilal thought equip-ping Jody with *that* was like giving a five-year-old an AK with a zillion rounds of ammunition.

"I can teach ya," Jody offered. "It one thing I good at. ...Ever does it with somebody else?"

"That's a pretty personal question."

Jody giggled. "Dat mean you did."

"It means it's none of your business."

"Dat *really* mean you did."

Bilal snagged a towel from the rusty bar. "Did you?"

"Dat a pretty personal question."

"You sure you're really retarded?"

Jody looked solemnly thoughtful. "Pretty sure most of da time 'cause people remind me a lot. ...Breakfast almost ready, den we fix Mr. Whatley's truck so's we can get your stuff."

"Aight," said Bilal.

"Hey, you just like Quentin... 'cept black."

"Yeah, I noticed. ...But it's all there."

"Did I say somethin' retarded?"

"Bein' honest ain't retarded, but sometimes you gotta be careful who you're bein' honest to."

"Friends can always be honest. Dat's what Quentin say. Wanna be my friend?"

Bilal smiled. "Sure."

"Goody! Now I gots three! ...I shouldn't of said goody, huh?"

Bilal patted Jody's shoulder. "That doesn't sound retarded to me."

On the kitchen table was a platter of hash-browns, crispy gold and fried just right. There was also a plate of sausage links, a steaming stack of buttered toast, and glasses of milk and orange juice. Quentin, bare-foot in only jeans, was tending a frying pan on the stove as Bilal, now also in jeans, followed Jody into the room. Outside the mist was thinning, and sunlight brightened the window. Distantly a rooster crowed, sounding just like on TV, and the bell of

Saint Toads clanked eight times.

"How you like your eggs?" asked Quentin.

Bilal took a chair. "Over medium."

"Two or three?"

"Three," said Bilal, grabbing a fork and stabbing links to load up a plate. "Eee, eee, eee!"

Jody laughed, "Three for me, too!" and piled his plate with potatoes.

"How come these eggs are orange?" asked Bilal.

"'Cause da chickens eats greens," said Jody. "On da Injun reservation. Dey run around all over da place 'stead of bein' locked in cages. Dat's how eggs s'posed ta look, not dem wussy yellow kind my aunt get down at Walmart. An' da milk is real, too, not dat milk-flavored water shit dey make you drink at school."

"So the Indians have organic farms?"

"Nah," said Jody, his mouth full of sausage. "It just da way dey always growed stuff, like before us white people came. Annie get her meat from dem; dat why her burgers rock."

Bilal ruffled the kid's oily hair and tried to ignore his goaty smell... Jody might have known ten different ways but none of them seemed to be in a shower. "You're not really retarded."

"Ambiguously."

Quentin sat down at the table. "Except when you're smokin'."

"Sorry I lost dat letter." Jody turned to Bilal. "It was a letter for you."

"That's cool," said Bilal. "I wouldn't have gotten it anyway." He salted and peppered his eggs, which were perfectly done with no runny spots. "You kick ass at cookin', cousin."

"Thanks, but Annie taught me."

Jody snagged a slice of toast and slathered it with blueberry jelly. "We gonna shoot some dirty rats?"

Quentin forked potatoes. "Maybe after we fix the truck."

"Rats spread disease," said Jody, turning to Bilal.

"So do monkeys," said Bilal.

"So do haters," said Quentin.

A half hour later the sun was bright in a clear blue sky and the channel was glistening emerald green. The morning air was growing hot as Bilal, clinging to Quentin, rode the back of the chugging Gote. Jody pedaled behind on his bike as they clattered through town with a tail of smoke. All the boys were shirtless, and Quentin had his shotgun tied across the handlebars.

Mr. Gilman was sweeping his porch beside the stack of addled pumpkins. He paused to smile and wave, and the boys waved back. A handful of pickups were at the cafe, and men in blue denim were eating inside at tables with red-and-white checkered cloths. A few other vehicles sat here and there in front of the few remaining stores that didn't have boards on their windows; and a woman was raising the American flag at the tiny, jail-like post office. Mr. Gilman stopped sweeping again to stand at respectful attention.

"So, you don't know where your grandfather is?" asked Quentin above the engine's beat.

"Not till he writes," said Bilal, pressing close to Quentin's ear. "But I guess he rented another house."

"He could *buy* a house here for next to nothin'. There's some cool ones along the channel, them ol' Victorian spooky kind, an' even got docks for boats. ...Ain't that one of the American dreams? Like, why he came here from Sudan?"

"He came here to get away from terror, but he only got the American flavor."

As Bilal had noticed last night on the bridge, there were more empty houses than people in Rust. Many had boards on their windows, and rotting picket fences around their weed-choked yards. He pictured his grandfather planting flowers and resurrecting a dead yellow lawn. Maybe even a garden in back. He could sit on his porch in the evenings without the scream of sirens, or stupid monkeys shoot-ing guns. And Bilal could... maybe get a boat. And a minibike.

"But, Jadd ain't on the under about bein' who he is."

"Yeah," said Quentin. "That might be hard for people to accept."

Bilal looked over his shoulder and saw a battered sheriff's Suburban, a dusty green-and-white 4X4, trailing Jody's bike. The truck had an ancient rotating light like a gumball machine on its roof, but it wasn't flashing; and the cop at the wheel only beeped the horn instead of blasting a siren. Bilal didn't know much about vehicle laws, but the Gote was probably breaking them all... even without the shotgun. "Quentin. There's a cop behind us."

Quentin brought the Gote to a stop in front of the boarded-up Rexall. The cop was a lanky but beer-bellied man in a tan uniform that looked second-hand with a faded American flag on his shoulder, though the star on his chest was proudly polished. A cowboy six-shooter rode on his hip, and he wore a Clint Eastwood hat. His steel-gray eyes skimmed Bilal but looked more curious than suspicious. "Mornin' Quentin. Gonna get rid of a few more rats? I'm uppin' the bounty to a dollar apiece."

"Mornin', Deputy Best," said Quentin. "Maybe later. Gonna fix Mr. Whatley's truck... probably needs a coil. Gotta haul a dresser an' book shelf."

"Don't let me see you drivin' it. Whatley ain't licensed that thing in years."

"I'll take the old stage road."

"Then I won't see you."

"This is my cousin Bilal," said Quentin. "He's gonna be stayin' with me awhile."

"That so?" said the man, regarding Bilal. "Cousin on your father's side? Guess he'd be your step-cousin."

Quentin shrugged. "Never thought about it."

"Don't know how that works myself when people been adopted." The man extended a hand. "Dalton Best."

Resisting an urge to say "Howdy, Sheriff," Bilal shook hands with the man. "Bilal Taimur."

"Nice to meet you, Bilal. You gonna be goin' to school?"

"Yes, sir, I registered yesterday."

"I knew your uncle, a real good man. Too bad about that bridge accident."

"Thanks," said Bilal.

"There's five generations of Bests in the graveyard an' I'm glad he's restin' with them."

"'Cept his head," piped Jody.

"Shut up!" snapped Quentin.

The deputy turned to Jody. "How's your aunt these days?"

"Full of shit."

The deputy patted Jody's shoulder. "Just hang in there, son. If there's a reason for all we go through we'll find it out on Judgment Day. ...Well, Quentin, you stay out of trouble. An' no more fights at Annie's." Best smiled when Quentin looked surprised. "Annie didn't rat you out, but word's got a habit of getting' around an' most of it finds me sooner or later."

"...Oh," said Quentin.

"Speakin' of Annie, got me a ten-pound cat in the reeds just north of her dock by the ol' hangin' tree."

"Cool," said Quentin. "We're goin' fishin' later."

"Good luck, Quentin. Bilal. Jody." The deputy started back to his truck, but paused and faced the boys again. "Any you seen an ol' Firebird? A '75 an' barbecue black? Driver's a red-haired kid dealin' drugs."

Bilal hesitated: hadn't he done the right thing enough? But finally he said, "I did, yesterday. On Channel Road. He tried to sell me a lot of shit."

"Thanks, Bilal. He's been sellin' to kids around schools, burger joints an' quickie-marts. An' Walmart down in Saunders Ferry. Some kid down there took somethin' of his an' he's in the hospital now."

Quentin was scanning Bilal, though his eyes, as always, were hidden. At last he said, "I seen him last week. In his car at Annie's after school let out."

"I seen him dere, too," said Jody. "Flagrantly."

"Thanks," said Best. "Real men protect their community, like gettin' rid of rats."

EIGHTEEN

"Um?" said Bilal, shirtless and barefoot like Jody and Quentin, and getting carefully into the boat, feeling like Sam the Hobbit, while Quentin, already aboard, primed the motor by pumping a hose. "Are there life-jackets?"

"Under the seat in the bow," said Quentin, pointing to some tattered orange things. "The bow is the front, the stern is the back. But just hang on to me if we sink."

Jody laughed on the dock, holding a trio of fishing poles, his feet, though mostly concealed by his cuffs, looking like a Hobbit's. "Yeah, he float like a raft."

"Can't you swim, Bilal?" asked Quentin.

Bilal sat down on the center seat, gripping it tight as Quentin's bulk rocked the little vessel. "Never got a chance to learn."

"I can teach ya," said Jody, bounding kid-like aboard. "Even a retard can swim."

"Don't call yourself names," growled Quentin. "There's plenty of assholes who'll do it for you." He pulled the starter handle and the motor sputtered to life. Jody untied the rope from a post, and Quentin twisted the throttle. The shabby orange boat swung away from the dock and churned beneath the bridge. Quentin twisted the throttle again, and the boat reared back like an eager horse and sped away down the channel.

Bilal hung onto the seat as the boat whooshed over the water. But after a while he relaxed and watched the reedy banks pass by as Quentin puffed a cigarette and Jody lounged in the bow. The sun felt good on his midnight skin, and silver spray tingled his chest. He fingered the charm as it bounced on its chain and swung between his bobbing breasts like a clapper slapping Jell-O bells and wished Devon was here. Did Allah have boats in Paradise? Did kids have fun up there? You wouldn't need any life-jackets... or safety belts in rusty old trucks, or helmets to ride a minibike.

Bilal had forgotten his fear, enjoying the splash and jounce of the boat and watching the wake as it swept through the reeds upsetting sleepy turtles on logs, by the time they were nearing Annie's dock, where Shawn, in only cutoff jeans and looking like a young elf prince with all his muscles and long golden hair, stood waiting with a fishing pole. His big blue eyes were curious as Quentin guided the boat to the dock and Jody threw the rope.

"That's your cousin?" he asked, after tying the rope to a post.

"Yeah," said Quentin. "His name's Bilal." He shut off the murmuring motor as the church bell gave a single clank.

Shawn offered a hand to Bilal. "So, that was you yesterday? I didn't figure you'd be *this* black. ...Um, yo, dog."

Jody giggled. "Don't try an' talk black, ya sound retarded."

"Need any help gettin' out?" asked Shawn, after shaking hands.

"Maybe a little."

Shawn helped Bilal onto the dock, then offered a hand to Quentin, who didn't seem to need it but took it anyway. "I ordered the grub when I saw you comin'."

Jody clambered out of the boat. "Tugboat Triples an' blueberry sundaes?"

"'Course."

"How's things at home?" asked Quentin, as Shawn tugged up his slipping jeans like an automatic thing.

"Same old shit. They want me back in sports an' I told 'em to piss up a rope. Like, what are sports anyhow? If you lose you get yelled at by a goon. If you win, the *goon* gets a trophy."

"Um?" asked Bilal. "How's your brother?"

Shawn laughed. "His balls still hurt, but he deserved it. I shoulda done that myself. ...An' I will if he hassles you."

Annie's voice boomed through the quiet air. "Tugboat Triple Specials!"

*   *   *

The bell of Saint Toads had clanked three times when Bilal felt a tug on his fishing pole. The boat was tied to the branch of an oak, a massive old tree that spread over the water and cooled the air with its leafy shade. Quentin, Shawn and Jody had already caught a lot of fish, but none of the dudes had ragged Bilal for coming up with jack. Bilal was still comfortably stuffed from lunch, and time had passed in quiet peace with only the drowsy rustle of reeds and the lapping of water along the boat, except when someone got a bite. Jody was on the bow seat, pole in hands but maybe asleep, his almost chinless chin on chest. Shawn and Quentin sat back-to-back on the wide rear seat, their feet spread over the water. It was hard to tell without seeing his eyes, but Quentin's expression seemed gentle whenever he looked at Shawn; and both had lost the tough-ass fronts they'd worn at Annie's yesterday.

"Wish you was here, man," whispered Bilal, thinking of Devon again, then... "Shit, I got a fish!"

"Goody!" yelled Jody, snapping awake. "Hey it a whopper!"

"Seriously!" yelled Shawn.

Quentin grabbed a net. "'Bout time, virgin!"

"What should I do?" yelped Bilal, as the pole whipped back and forth in his hands and the reel unwound with a squeal.

"Reel him in!" yelled Shawn.

"But not too fast!" warned Jody as Bilal began to crank the reel. "Or you bust da line!"

The line sliced hissing through the water, the pole bending into an upside-down U. Quentin shouted, "Don't let him dive!"

"Or he go under dem roots!" yelled Jody.

Bilal was suddenly pouring sweat, fighting the fish, cranking the reel. "One of you wanna take over?"

"Nah, he's yours," said Shawn.

A monster catfish broke the surface, black as polished ebony, its underbelly white as snow. Jody capered like a kid. "That a goddamn whale!"

Quentin leaned out with a net, while Shawn and Jody balanced the boat by scrambling to the other side. "Got him!"

"Cool!" puffed Bilal, shaking sweat from his eyes.

Jody laughed. "Dat gonna be your dinner tanight."

"...All of it? But it's huge!"

"You catch it, you eat it," said Shawn. "It's one of the rules."

"Fried in cornmeal," added Quentin. "An' served on a bed of buttered rice with some herbs an' spices. I'll make home-fries, too." He held out a burlap sack, and Bilal dropped the fish inside.

"How many we got?" asked Shawn.

"Enough for a couple of dinners, an' some for Annie an' Mr. Gilman."

"Now we goes swimmin'," said Jody. "We gotta teach Bilal."

Shawn gave Bilal an amazed look. "You can't swim?"

Quentin dipped the sack in the channel to wet it again and keep the fish cool. "He never got a chance to learn."

Shawn shook his head. "Livin' in a city must suck."

"Seriously," agreed Bilal.

"So let's go ta McElligot's Pool," said Jody.

"Um..." said Bilal. "I don't got swimmin' trunks."

Jody laughed. "Nobody does at McElligot's Pool."

"It's one of the rules," said Shawn.

Quentin pulled the starter as Jody untied the boat from the tree. Watching the kid unwinding the rope reminded Bilal of something. "This used to be a hangin' tree? Like for bandits an' outlaws?"

"Mostly Indians," said Shawn, settling next to Quentin again. "There used to be a bounty on 'em, twenty dollars a head, dead. 'Course, that was just the men, an' older boys like us."

"...Why?"

"'Cause they was in the way. First when the gold miners came, then when people started farmin'."

"Did they scalp people?"

"They weren't that kind of tribe," said Shawn. "Never made wars or massacred people. Mostly hunted rabbits an' deer, an' fished in the rivers an' creeks. But some of 'em used to steal cattle after us white people came, 'cause there weren't nothin' to hunt no more; an' my great-great-grand-father shot one for stealin' some corn in the winter... 'course I ain't proud of that."

"What about the women an' kids?"

"Without the men most of 'em starved."

Bilal looked up at the huge oak tree, which must have stood there for hundreds of years. Maybe Indian kids had climbed in its branches and fished underneath in its friendly shade? It was a beautiful thing, but people had used it to kill other people. And people had made other people suffer by letting women and children starve. Hadn't they read their Bible?

Quentin said, "But now they got a reservation."

"An' most of 'em are fat," said Jody. "So dey ain't starvin'. Obviously."

"An' they're buildin' a casino," said Shawn. "Which might even save the town."

"But da tree is haunted!" said Jody. "So don't never come here at night!"

"Guess it would be," said Bilal, gazing back at the ancient oak as Quentin turned the boat around and headed for the bridge.

NINETEEN

"There really *was* a McElligot? An' he had a pool?"

Shawn smiled at Bilal, his shoulder pressed to Quentin's as the boat wooshed up the channel. "That's what everybody calls it. Even my dad when he was a kid."

They had passed under the bridge again, and Quentin had docked at the house to put the fish in the fridge. Now he slowed the bouncing boat and turned it toward a grove of trees along the reedy shore. The trees were weeping willows and almost hid the mouth of a stream that flowed into the channel. Jody stood in the bow, pushing the dangling branches aside as the boat glided into a creek or brook... Bilal wasn't sure of the difference. The water was still beneath the trees, a dark and glossy green. Jody ducked a bigger branch and pointed through the leaves. "Da graveyard over dere, Bilal. You could see your uncle's grave."

"Yeah, if you wanna," said Quentin, guiding the boat around moss-covered roots and into a tunnel of leaf-dappled shade. It looked like a natural mosque in a forest, with an arching roof of willow leaves and massive beams of living wood. The leaves were gold and green, and sunlight filtered softly down as if though stained-glass windows. "Maybe after swimmin'."

"...Yeah," said Bilal, though he wasn't sure about swimming. But he felt kind of trapped, not wanting these dudes to think he was scared. Then, above the motor's purr, he heard kid-laughter, and then a big splash. He peered over Jody's shoulder: ahead was an almost circular pool. It was maybe thirty feet across, and the mammoth willows shaded the water except for a shaft of sun in the center. The banks were lined with ranks of reeds and carpeted with

117

long green grass. The place looked even more like a mosque, as if what they'd come through was only a hall; though off to his right through curtains of leaves he caught a few glimpses of weathered tombstones.

Then, a shock ran though him when he saw a pair of naked girls! Both were enormously rolly fat with skin like burnished copper and long raven hair almost down to their waists. One was wading up to the bank among the glossy reeds, the other swinging from a rope that dangled from a branch. She let go of the rope in the shaft of sun and made another massive splash. But a second later Bilal realized they were the Indian *boys*, the twins he'd seen yesterday at Annie's; and parked on the shore were their ATVs.

Both of them seemed to go tense as Quentin cut the motor and the boat glided into the pool. The boy in the water swam a few strokes, graceful despite all his weight, then waded to backup his brother, both watching with wary expressions as Quentin and posse invaded their space. Bilal looked back at Quentin, wondering if the bully show was going to start again, but Quentin only raised a hand in the universal sign of peace. Bilal almost expected a "how," but Quentin called "hey" instead.

The Indian boys still looked wary, like wild things in a nature show when predators were near. Both flicked glances to their machines as if judging how much time it would take to get to them and bail. Then Bilal saw rifles strapped to the handlebars; ancient cowboy carbines with feathers tied to their barrels. He remembered a History Channel show: the guns were antique 30-30s, called Yellow Boys by the Indians because of their brass receivers. Maybe the dudes were thinking of payback rather than running away?

Then Shawn called, "hey." Then Jody. The twins exchanged un-certain looks but seemed to relax a little. Still, they moved back a few paces, deeper into leafy shade -- also closer to their guns -- as the boat nosed gently onto the bank and Jody hopped out with the rope.

"Hey," called Quentin again. "It's cool." The guns didn't seem to bother him. "Sorry about yesterday."

The twins didn't seem convinced that Quentin had come to smoke a peace pipe, but they gave Bilal curious looks, then crossed their arms over their chest balloons. They looked like lessons in drawing cartoons where every shape was an oval or sphere, including their bottoms like huge copper moons. Both were leaning drastically backwards to balance their gigantic bellies, which avalanched to their dimpled knees, their navels like tunnels into night, big enough to swallow baseballs, and far below the reach of their hands. Bilal wasn't good at guessing weights but they must have been quarter-ton kids.

"Yeah?" asked one. "Then why did you do it?"

"Yeah!" echoed the other. "You owe us Tugboat Triples!"

"An' blueberry sundaes!" added his brother.

"Okay," said Quentin.

Bilal smiled. "Hope you're not speakin' with a forked tongue."

The twins relaxed and laughed. "Yeah, we know all about that," said one.

The other waddled up to Bilal as he stepped ashore behind Jody, his mammoth thighs getting in each other's way so he still seemed to be wading, and heaving his bulk from side to side like a huge copper penguin. "Black man help white man kill red man."

"Oh shut up," said his brother. "That makes you sound retarded."

"Can't we all just go swimmin'?" said Jody.

"Um?" asked Bilal, remembering why they were here. "Is it hard?"

The twins laughed again. "Is what hard?" asked one.

"He don't know how to swim," said Quentin, also climbing out of the boat after taking Shawn's offered hand.

"Huh?" exclaimed the twins together. They turned their eyes to Bilal again as if he'd rolled up on a camel.

"This is my cousin Bilal," said Quentin.

The twins looked puzzled, and then one said, "Like, on your father's side."

"He's from a city," added Shawn. "Never got a chance to swim."

"That's gotta suck," said the other twin.

"Seriously," said Bilal, though he wished Shawn hadn't said that. It was like, the more friendly you got with people the harder it was to hide who you were.

"It's zombie-easy," said one of the twins.

119

"I'm Chucky," said his brother.

"I'm Bucky," added his clone.

Bilal couldn't resist; he held up a palm and said, "how."

"Wuttup, dawg," said Bucky.

"We know how," said Chucky, cupping a fist and making sign language.

Bilal wondered how they could *find* themselves under all that pendulous fat, but it wouldn't be cool to ask.

"We all know how," said Jody. "So, 'less you wanna circle-jerk, can't we all go swimmin'?"

Bucky made a solemn face. "Circle-jerk sacred ceremony only for blood brothers."

"Really?" asked Bilal.

Chucky laughed. "Nah, but I'm in the mood for swimmin'."

"...Oh," said Bilal, who pictured a cartoonish scene from the Disney movie, *Peter Pan*, with all The Lost Boys in their animal suits gathered in a leafy glade while Goat-Boy taught them ten different ways. Though he'd never done a "ceremony" with anyone but Devon, it seemed like a better idea than swimming.

"So, what we waitin' for?" said Jody. He tied the boat's rope to a tree branch, then slipped out of his jeans. As Bilal had almost expected, he was faun-like furry below the waist; and it wouldn't have been a big surprise if he'd conjured Pan pipes and started to jam.

Shawn and Quentin shed their jeans, and after a moment Bilal did, too.

"Woah!" said Chucky, scoping Bilal, who expected a comment about his equipment, but Bucky said:

"You're seriously black all over!"

"I noticed," said Bilal, and wondered again how they could do it... maybe by telekinesis? "Um, don't you got Indian names?"

"Oh sure," said Chucky. "I'm Shitting Bear an' he's Farting Fox."

Bucky laughed. "Just punkin'. Our great-great grandfather got Christianized... at least the white-eyes thought he was."

Chucky added, "He figured it was smarter 'cause the Christian god had guns."

"Now He's got pancake breakfasts," said Bucky. "All you can eat every Sunday."

"An' our tribe's got money," said Chucky. "We're buildin' a casino."

"Can you speak Indian?" asked Bilal.

"Can you speak African?" asked Bucky.

"C'mon dammit!" cried Jody. He grabbed Bilal's hand with a furry paw and pulled him toward the water. Bilal was scared again, but found himself surrounded by a gang of cheerful naked dudes, all urging him into the emerald pool as if he was going to be baptized. The water was cool in the afternoon heat as Jody towed him through the reeds. In moments he was up to his chest and Jody up to his neck. The Indian boys were floating near like copper-colored walrus cubs, the balloons of their chests bobbing under their chins. Quentin was also afloat a little farther out in the sun, with Shawn holding onto his shoulder.

"...So... what now?" asked Bilal when finally up to his own neck.

"Start swimmin'!" said Jody. "Like dis!" He paddled away like a dog. ...Or maybe a goat, if goats could swim.

Chucky and Bucky flanked Bilal. "Grab onto us if you sink," said Bucky, though Bilal wasn't sure which was which.

"Yeah," said Chucky. "We got your back."

Despite the boys around him, it took more courage than facing a gang of AK-packing monkeys. Sucking a breath, Bilal launched himself into deeper water. For a moment he spluttered and thrashed, but Jody and the twins were there, supporting him and shouting advice; and swimming wasn't really hard once he got the idea. And his chub kept him afloat. Soon he was paddling by himself with everybody cheering.

Then he seemed to lose track of time, there in that watery natural mosque with his friends praising God, not knowing they were, in a rowdy savage innocence that holy men who prayed to Him would never understand. *We have given you clothing with which to cover your nakedness, and garments pleasing to the eye, but the finest of all these is the robe of piety.*

Soon he was swinging from the rope, to land with a splash in the water, plunging deep into cool green space then kicking once more into leaf-dappled light to paddle ashore and do it again, and helping Shawn and Quentin boost Chucky and Bucky into the tree. Bilal was surprised when the bell of Saint Toads, like a cranky old muezzin clearing his throat, clanked six times in the distance.

The sun was getting low in the west, and shadows were deepening under the trees as the boys all gathered again on the shore. The twins helped each other into their jeans -- as much as could fit, which wasn't a lot -- then to put on each other's sneaks, since both were too fat to reach their own feet. Quentin called to them as Shawn helped him tug up his jeans. "Wanna come over for supper? Catfish an' home-fries."

"Cool," said Chucky.

"Cool," echoed Bucky, and pulled a phone from a pocket. "I'll tell mom we won't be home for dinner."

Chucky produced an identical phone. "I'll tell dad." Then he added to Quentin, "You still owe us Tugboat triples."

Jody laughed, clean for the first time since Bilal had met him, smelling now of earth and trees, with leaves entangled in his hair. "With swab-bucket fries an' tanker Cokes."

"An' blueberry sundaes," added Bilal.

"Seriously," said Shawn.

"Meet us at my house," said Quentin. "Go in an' watch TV till we get there."

"Got cable?" asked Chucky.

"Yeah, an' help yourselves to what's in the fridge."

"Peace," said the twins together, and mounted their motorized ponies.

"Can you stop at the store?" asked Quentin. "Get a gallon of milk, a pound of butter, an' whatever you want for dessert. Put it on my tab."

"Chocolate cream pies?" asked Bucky.

"Cool."

The ATVs snarled to life, and the boys popped wheelies, spraying dirt and roaring away, their long hair scattering water drops and flying free behind. Bilal almost expected a pair of *woos!* but maybe that would have been lame.

"Wanna see the grave?" asked Quentin.

"Yeah," said Bilal.

The sun was crowning the top of a hill as they pushed through a curtain of willow leaves and came to a little graveyard along the channel bank. Wading waist-deep through dry yellow weeds, they wound their way past time-weathered crosses and mossy, tilted tombstones. Many were crumbling marble or granite, others of iron eaten by rust, and a few of ancient rotting wood like those in cowboy movies. On many the years had erased the names, but there seemed to be a lot of Bests, a group of Gilmans, a row of Whatleys, a line of Wickets and several Skellys, along with a grander group of Rusts. Bilal didn't know Shawn's family name, but the blond boy paused for a moment as they passed a huddle of crosses. Finally they came to a small marble stone, still shiny and mostly unweathered. The long grassy mound at its foot hadn't sunk and seemed to be recently tended.

"I pull the weeds," said Quentin.

Bilal wasn't sure what to do, never having met the man whose skull-less skeleton lay below; but Quentin knelt by the grave, so Bilal knelt beside him.

"The town bought that," said Quentin, indicating the stone. "An' paid all the expenses. The coffin was coffin-shaped. Made of wood, an' had brass handles. ... 'Course, it was closed at the funeral."

Bilal read the chiseled inscription, which included REST IN PEACE. "Guess he changed his name to Tanner?"

Quentin brushed dust from the stone, which was classically shaped with a rounded top. "Not officially, that's just what everybody thought. Reverend Bray wanted to give him a cross, but my brother an' me talked him out of it."

"Was he was still Faithful?" asked Bilal.

"Inside he was, where it probably counts. I thought about changin' the name to Taimur... I got a hammer an' chisel. Nobody would probably notice." Then he lowered his voice, as if the other dead might hear. "Think I should?"

"I don't know." Bilal looked around at the other graves, mostly

Christian he supposed… at least they'd been buried that way. "But, maybe they know."

"Don't look like it bother 'em," said Jody.

"Yeah," said Shawn. "Like, nobody started a skeleton war about whose god is better."

Jody said, "Maybe dead people don't hate each other." He looked at the golden sky overhead. "Think God fixes people up dere? Like, makes 'em smart an' cool lookin' when det retarded an' ugly like me?"

"You're not ugly!" snapped Quentin.

"An' only a little retarded," said Shawn.

Bilal touched Jody's arm. "You're cooler than most of the people I met in ways that really matter." He also lifted his eyes to the sky and his tone was like a challenge. "People who hate don't go to heaven, no matter how good they think they are!"

The sun had vanished behind the hills and the sky was turning rose and pink as the boys returned to the boat. Shawn helped Quentin climb in, and Bilal hopped easily aboard as if he'd been around boats all his life. Shawn and Jody pushed off from the bank as Quentin pulled the starter. Jody stood in the bow again, parting the curtains of willow leaves as they churned away toward the channel, while Shawn joined Quentin in the stern. Bilal gazed back as they left the pool, which was lit by a lingering rosy glow as if by unseen candles. It really did look like a mosque, and one that God, not man, had made.

"On whose name be praise," he whispered.

TWENTY

Devon?" Bilal opened his eyes to the dim red glow of the warning light on the bridge. The mist had risen again and slowly swirled against the windows where ruby droplets beaded the glass. The scent of Devon was strong in his nose, but his cheek was pillowed on Devon's jacket. Again, like the bell of a sunken ship came the lonely call of the church.

Bilal counted twelve dead-sounding clanks, but found he was throbbing with life. Easing onto his back, he reached over his belly, still full from a feast of corn-mealed catfish deliciously fried in butter and served on snowy beds of rice with mountains of crispy golden home-fries, and wedges of chocolate cream pie for dessert. Then they had sprawled in the living room, overloading the ratty old couch and sharing a family-size bag of chips along with two sixers of beer, their feet spread bare on the coffee table, watching *House Of A Thousand Corpses*... Bilal pointing out the Agatha Crispies and getting laughter from everyone. Chucky and Bucky had left around ten, and Jody a little while later. Bilal had gone to bed soon after, tired from all the day's adventures.

Now, lying here in the red-tinted darkness, he wanted another of life's good things. Unlike Quentin's creaky crib, the iron cot wouldn't betray him, but he'd still have to go easy. He flicked a glance to Quentin's bed, but Quentin wasn't there. Was he was still with Shawn watching TV? Bilal listened a moment but heard no sounds. Maybe he'd gone to the bathroom? Bilal didn't want to be interrupted; the night was warm despite the mist, and he could go down to the dock.

He eased from the cot and stood up, then opened the door and descended the stairs, his onyx shaft protruding from its puff of chub below his belly as if eagerly pointing the way. The mist surrounded him warm and moist, and the moss on the dock was soft underfoot. Should he do it in the boat? That would be something new: it might even count as an eighth different way.

He got in the boat and lay down in the bottom, his legs spread over the center seat, his back against the stern's. Applying the requisite fingers and thumb, he closed his eyes and began, his belly and chest jiggling rhythmically. For a moment he dreamily pictured himself in leaf-dappled light in the grass by the pool while Jody sat playing a flute. But maybe the music was only the breeze as it sighed through the willows and rustled the reeds.

Then he let his mind drift to make its own movie, but after a mom-ent he opened his eyes. There was something he'd seen but hadn't noticed coming out of the house, a feeling he often got in the 'hood when reminding himself to watch his back. Above him, red-lit by the warning lamp, the bridge tower loomed against the sky, vanishing upward into the mist. On the edge of sight was a greenish blur from the traffic light over the road, but now he noticed a dim golden glow: the windows in the control house.

Was Quentin up there, he wondered? Maybe he was fixing some-thing, oiling up those rusty gears or cleaning off the spider webs? ...Well, it was none of his business. He closed his eyes to start again, but found himself thinking of Quentin alone among all that massive machinery.

A few minutes later and puffing a bit, Bilal reached the top of the ladder. The traffic light cast its greenish glow beneath the iron plat-form, but the town and the land were shrouded in mist. He couldn't see the house below or the top of the tower above. It was like he'd climbed halfway to somewhere... between heaven and earth like it said in books. He went to open the control house door, but stopped when he heard soft voices inside. He shouldn't have worried; Shawn was with Quentin.

Again, he almost lifted the latch, but something told him not to. Instead he went to a window and peeped through one of the little square panes. ...For a second a shock rippled though him. It was like when he'd first seen Chucky and Bucky and thought they were naked girls. Shawn and Quentin were hugging, Shawn's muscular body in Quentin's arms, Shawn likewise embracing Quentin's bulk, pressing tightly chest-to-chest.

...Well, they were friends, Bilal told himself. And Shawn had stayed close to Quentin all day, doing a million little things like pulling up Quentin's slipping jeans, offering a helping hand, things that any good friend would do. Bilal and Devon had hugged a lot...

But they'd never gone as far as a kiss.

Bilal only watched for a moment, then drew away into the mist. A mix of feelings jumbled his mind: there was a sudden physical need for something he'd been dreaming of, even if not with another boy, a new wave of warmth flooding his body, perhaps a stab of ambiguous envy, and then a flash of shame that he felt it. Last came a pang of loneliness, of seeing light and... love... so close and yet an infinity out of his reach.

The physical heat quickly died, and for a moment he shivered, cold and alone in the dark. Then, from the mist came another soft voice. "Explains a lot of things, huh?"

Bilal turned around. Devon was sitting on the rail like a rolly-poly cherub, smiling like he always did. "Yeah," said Bilal in a low tone. He pointed to the warm-lit window. "Is this what it's like for you, man, bein' outside lookin' in?"

Devon looked sad. "Yeah."

Bilal raised a hand toward the sky. "So, go on, Devon, like in *Ghost*. You're done with all the shit down here, an' you can see the light."

Devon smiled again. "I can also see you catchin' a fish an' learnin' how to swim."

"An' jackin' off in a boat?"

Devon laughed. "Maybe you should axe Jody to teach you new ways."

Bilal pointed skyward again. "Maybe they do all that stuff up there. An' don't forget the virgins."

Devon shrugged. "They can wait."

"S'cuse me for askin' but..."

"Bein' dead kinda takes me outta the mood. 'Course, maybe that's 'cause I'm still new at it."

"Sure you can't read my mind?"

"Nah, I just know how you think."

"Is it 'cause you died too soon... why you don't wanna go to the light?"

"You're the expert on ghosts."

Bilal wondered if he could hug Devon now and feel his friendly warmth again. But, maybe he shouldn't try: if his arms found only nothing he would know he was alone. "Was Jody right?" he asked, and turned to gaze up at the tower. "About God fixin' people up there?"

"Think there was somethin' wrong with me?"

"Only you were too good for the 'hood. ...Like, you were a light an' that's what they hated."

"Maybe a few people gotta be lights or everybody would be in the dark."

TWENTY-ONE

"Wanna go to church with me?"

Bilal opened his eyes to pale sunlight. The mist was slowly thinning outside, and Quentin was standing by the cot in only droopy jeans. "You go to church?" asked Bilal.

"I help Annie cook pancakes. But they don't got a Muslim detector, an' they ain't gonna splash you with holy water to see if you melt like in *Devil's Rain.*"

"What do they do?"

"Sing a few old-fashioned songs. Then Reverend Bray preaches a little; 'love your neighbor' an' that kinda stuff. The best part is havin' breakfast 'cause people feel good when they're eatin' together."

"I... guess it would be okay," said Bilal, "but I only got T-shirts to wear."

"I got a few old button shirts way too small for me now."

"Aight," said Bilal, getting up. His mind was a little fuzzy from sleep, and he wondered if he'd only dreamed climbing the bridge and what he'd seen. ...But there was rust on his hands from the ladder. Then he noticed a strand of long golden hair entangled in Quentin's curly mop. Quentin had gone to his dresser and was rummaging in a drawer. Bilal came over and touched his shoulder. "I think I know why you an' Shawn started actin' so bad this summer."

"What you mean?" demanded Quentin. He spun around to face Bilal like he'd spun to face his attackers.

Bilal almost stepped back, but then stood his ground. "I saw you up on the bridge last night. ...Not on purpose. I came up to see if you were okay."

129

"...Oh," said Quentin, his brawny shoulders sagging a bit.

"I think it's cool," said Bilal. He drew the strand of golden hair from Quentin's dusky curls. "I could see you love each other. ...But, I kinda guessed that already, even if I didn't know it."

"How?" demanded Quentin, squaring his shoulders again.

"Just a lot of little things. But most people wouldn't notice."

It was hard to tell without seeing his eyes, but Quentin might have looked relieved. But then his voice hardened. "It ain't cool in this town!" He snatched the strand of hair from Bilal and shoved it into his pocket like something a little kid would do.

Bilal spread his hands. "But, most of the people here seem good."

"Most of 'em are." Quentin pulled a blue chambray shirt from the drawer and gave it to Bilal. "But, they're just," He shrugged. "People. An' life ain't a Disney movie where people suddenly see a light an' stop hatin' things they were taught to hate."

He found another shirt that was probably triple-X, then faced Bilal again. "Shawn's parents don't understand nothin' like that. They won't even try an' understand why he dropped out of sports. They think there's somethin' wrong with him... been talkin' about a private school 'to get him back on track.' An' that's just 'cause he won't play games: what you think they'd do if he told 'em he was...?"

Quentin made a face. "I don't even *like* that word! Makes me think of elves in tights prancin' around a Christmas tree!"

Bilal tried to picture Shawn in tights, but saw him riding a wolf instead. "His parents think somethin's wrong with him 'cause they don't know the truth."

Quentin snorted. "That's just more movie bullshit! The truth don't stop assholes from hatin'."

"I noticed that," said Bilal. "But, what about Jody?"

"I never lied to him in my life. He just don't know about me an' Shawn."

"But you're lyin' to him now," said Bilal. "Even if it ain't with words."

"What's that s'posed to mean?"

"You been his role-model all his life, an' now he's actin' like a bully 'cause you an' Shawn been frontin' bad... thinkin' it makes you look manly, I guess... so people won't suspect anything. He's suffered enough already, man; he don't need another reason for assholes to make him suffer."

"I didn't ask to be his role-model!"

"That's what stupid thug-rappers say when kids act like monkeys because of their songs. Most of those kids are lookin' for men because they never knew any. Men who ain't scared to be gentle an' kind. ...Men who ain't scared to be lights."

Bilal glanced at *Islam For Idiots* on the box by Quentin's bed. "'Did Allah not find thee an orphan and give thee shelter and care? And He found thee wandering, and He gave thee guidance.' That's what you done for Jody, man. That's what real men do. An' I saw two real men yesterday when we were fishin' an' swimmin'. An' makin' peace with people."

"What did you see on the bridge?" asked Quentin.

"The same real men bein' real."

Quentin seemed to consider, but then his face turned troubled. "Is it... um... obvious?"

"That you an' Shawn love each other? Probably not. ...Or just not yet."

"...You mean about girls? Like datin' an' stuff?"

"Maybe not this year," said Bilal. "But what about in ninth grade? Or tenth? You dudes gonna front about that, too? Lie to girls an' mess up their lives pretending you're somethin' you ain't?"

Quentin slammed the drawer. "You gonna start wearin' a kufi?"

"That ain't the same thing."

Quentin scowled again. "'Cause you ain't sure about what you believe so you don't feel bad about hidin' it? But, what if you really knew who you were an' what you really believed in? Would you let your 'light' shine then, knowin' you were gonna get hated?"

"I... don't know," said Bilal.

Quentin shrugged. "It don't matter for you: in a few months you'll be gone. Then you can be whoever you are."

TWENTY-TWO

Chucky sprawled back in an old metal chair that looked about ready to crumple. The balloons of his chest strained his red T-shirt as if about to bust the cloth as he gently massaged his mammoth belly, which spilled half bare in the morning sunlight and avalanched over his wide-spread legs. Bucky, dressed the same as his brother – or as much as boys of their bulk *could* be dressed -- including a necklace of little sea shells, also stroked his coppery blubber and challenged after a burp, "Bet I can eat another one."

Chucky blasted a bigger burp. "Bet I can eat *two* other ones."

"Want me to get 'em?" asked Bilal, whose own belly bulged full of heavenly pancakes slathered with butter and maple syrup created by Annie and Quentin on a wood-fired griddle under a tree.

"Yeah, please," sighed Bucky. "I'm too stuffed to move."

"One, or two?"

"Three," said Chucky and Bucky together.

"It's *sinful!*" squalled a woman's voice that sounded like nails being ripped from a board.

"My aunt gots da spirit again," sighed Jody, who was dressed in his Sunday best of faded jeans and a white T-shirt... close to being white, anyway. He might have actually taken a shower, though still emanated a randy scent suggesting a session of loving himself before being dragged by his aunt to love Jesus.

Bilal looked across the church's lawn, which was weedy and dotted with dandelions but a lot more alive than the school's. A dozen long tables had been set up, and most of the town seemed to be there, including Mr. Gilman and Deputy Dalton Best. Most of the

132

younger kids and teens were sitting with their families, but the twins had joined Bilal and Jody at a smaller table near the grill.

Bilal saw the witch from *The Wizard Of Oz*... except for not being green. She was stalking Reverend Bray, a plump pink man in a rusty black suit with a cross like an anti-vampire charm... though it didn't seem to work on witches. The woman pointed to the church: its doors were flanked by shocks of corn and a pair of psychotic but smiling pumpkins.

"Those are symbols of *Satan!*"

Reverend Bray smiled patiently, as if being annoyed by an amateur demon who had no power to trouble his soul. He must have been a *little* holy or he might have dunked Jody's aunt in the channel to see if she floated like a witch or sank like a true Christian should... which didn't make sense to Bilal because Jesus had walked on water. The man hadn't thundered a sermon in church, instead only quietly quoting the Bible... at least a few of the peaceful parts about loving your neighbor like Quentin had said.

Now the Reverend said cheerfully, "They're symbols of the harvest. Of food put away for the winter and thanks to the Lord that none will be hungry." He looked around at the cheerful people eating under the golden sun. "They're thanks that we have an abundance to share with our brothers and sisters, the *real* meaning of Trick Or Treat."

"It's Satan's celebration of *sin!*" the woman squalled in return. "And people *should* go hungry to remind them how Jesus suffered for us!" She glared around at the people, many of whom were super-size, including most of the Indian families. "Gluttony is a *sin!*"

"She's got the 'spirit' of somethin'," said Chucky.

"Like that guy in *The Shining*," said Bucky.

Reverend Bray sat down at a table and buttered his heavenly pancakes. "Jesus suffered in hope that we wouldn't. But He seldom refused a good meal, and provided many meals for others... loaves and fishes come to mind. He knew being hungry makes it hard to be thankful to God. Or to love one-another."

He reached for a bottle of syrup. "The real sin of gluttony is often misinterpreted, and the biggest misunderstanding is thinking it only applies to food." He ate a forkful of pancake, then regarded his ample middle, where the cross lay horizontally. "It's not the 'fat man' who won't go to heaven, but rather the *greedy* man who won't share; the 'rich man,' to quote the Bible, who allows or forces others to starve while hoarding his own abundance."

He ate another bite of pancake. "Gluttony comes in many disguises, and most have nothing to do with food. One may be a glutton of health, when outward appearance is worshiped and becomes more important than God. When the body becomes an earthly idol instead of a home for a spiritual soul."

He reached for another pat of butter. "Some people are gluttons of possessions, while others are gluttons of money or power." He might have glanced at Shawn's family. "Some parents are gluttons of their children, demanding too many accomplishments than should be expected of a child, mentally or physically. Or preaching their own beliefs or behaviors instead of giving their children the knowledge to make the right choices in life for themselves."

His mild blue eyes met the woman's. "And, there are gluttons of suffering... especially when it's perceived as a penance."

"Dat's my aunt," said Jody. "She say I make her suffer, but she sure seem ta like it."

Bucky patted his shoulder. "No wonder you're a little retarded."

"I think I'm gettin' better 'cause I don't listen to her no more."

Chucky laughed. "How can she hate Halloween so much an' still act like she rides a broom."

Bilal went to the grill where Quentin, in one of Annie's aprons, was flipping golden pancakes. Quentin hadn't said much since they'd ridden to church. Bilal had expected curious looks and wasn't surprised when he got them. But Quentin explained his presence, and nobody seemed to think it was strange that Quentin would have a black cousin; though word had apparently gotten around, maybe from Deputy Best.

Reverend Bray had welcomed him and seemed on the real about it. Bilal and Quentin had sat in a pew and shared a tattered book of hymns. The songs, like the sermon, were basically good, though he wondered if people really believed and actually tried to live by those words. When the congregation was called to pray Bilal had turned toward the east, though only Quentin noticed. Bilal had tried to think of Allah, but found himself picturing Devon instead, perched in the rafters and smiling down like one of those chubby angel kids.

Shawn had sat with his family; his father a lanky cowboy type in western shirt and bolo tie. His mother was thin but attractive, and Shawn had obviously gotten her hair, but she looked a little troubled whenever Shawn turned to Quentin. Shawn's father would openly frown, and Chris, his older brother, seemed more pissed at Quentin for being liked by Shawn than at Bilal for the kick in the balls. Jody had tried to sit with Quentin, but his aunt had snatched him away and seemed to take gluttonous pleasure in nastily twisting his arm.

Now, at the grill, Quentin looked up as Bilal brought the plates. "How many?" he asked.

"Three each," said Bilal, "for Chucky an' Bucky. I'm totally stuffed; your pancakes rock. Ever think of bein' a cook?"

Quentin loaded the plates. "Annie's gonna retire someday."

Bilal glanced at Annie, who was stirring a bowl of batter while humming a song that wasn't a hymn. "I didn't mean to piss you off. It wasn't none my business."

Quentin sighed. "It's cool, Bilal, I ain't pissed at you. I been thinkin' about what you said... even if bein' real ain't easy." His eyes were hidden as always, but he might have looked at Shawn, who was leaving with his family, who seemed to surround him like guards. Then he flipped a pancake and smiled.

"Wanna go swimmin' again today? An' I'll teach you to drive the Gote. Then we can get a burger at Annie's. An' there's a movie tonight, the original *Night Of The Living Dead.*"

"There's a theater in Rust?"

"Yeah, the Moonview. Wanna go?"

"Zombie cool," said Bilal.

TWENTY-THREE

Bilal had seen the movie twice but hadn't told his friends because some first-times were better when shared. It was one of the all-time zombie classics, and also the first American film in which a black man had played a part, not because he was black, but because he'd been the best man for the role.

The Moonview was sort of a zombie itself, like a huge rotting corpse that hadn't been buried; a big weedy lot that had once been graveled, where rusty posts with corroded speakers tottered like tombstones above ancient graves. Paint peeled like scabs from the sheet-metal screen, which looked about ready to topple; the cinder block projection booth was like an old crypt half sunk in the dirt; and the snack bar looked like the Crypt Keeper's kitchen where mice had gnawed the candy bars and some of the Raisinettes probably weren't. The burgers were mummified microwaved messes with shriveled slabs of mystery meat, and the cheeseburgers oozed yellow slime. The pizza looked recycled, the hot dogs like penises out of a morgue; and whatever they put on the "buttered" popcorn had not been created by a cow. The choice of drinks were crappy cola or something a nasty chemical orange that tasted like a petroleum product. It was no surprise that most of the trash being tossed out the windows of cars and trucks were burger wrappings and such from Annie's despite a peeling sign at the gate: NO OUTSIDE FOOD ALLOWED. Someone must have cleaned up now and then, but sun-rotted panties dangled from posts and crackly condoms littered the ground.

There were maybe a hundred speaker posts, though some were missing speakers, but less than thirty vehicles were parked among the weeds. Most were typical teenage cars, some with dusty Walmart wheels and J.C. Whitney accessories. About a third were four-by-four pickups, plus several dually flatbeds. These were facing away from the screen, their drivers and posses sprawled in back on bales of hay or patio chairs, and all equipped with coolers of beer. The clink of empties hitting the ground accompanied the movie sounds, along with yells and werewolf howls, while ruby embers glowed in the dark. The scents of tobacco and compost-class weed mingled with malty fumes of brew and an occasional whiff of piss from kids too drunk to bother with bathrooms... which held their own kind of horrors. Several cars rocked on squeaky springs whenever the action slowed on the screen.

Despite the trailer-trash atmosphere and middle-school mentality of a kiddie matinee in a wrecking yard, Bilal was enjoying the night. He felt like it was one of those first-times he might remember all his life. Like catching a fish and riding a boat and learning to swim in McElligot's Pool. Or helping Jody carve his pumpkin and seeing the genuine joy in his eyes when it came to life with a candle inside.

Bilal had driven the Gote tonight with Quentin riding behind, another first-time experience with the wind in his face, his dreads flying free, and the engine throbbing between his legs. Shawn had arrived on a dirt-bike just as they were leaving the house, and Jody had ridden with him. Chucky and Bucky had hooked up at Annie's, mount-ed on their ATVs, their Yellow Boys still on the handlebars, and packing two six-packs of Coke. Quentin had bought them the burgers he owed, then all had stocked up with grub for the movie... the candy at Annie's was half the price of the mouse-infested Moonview spew. Then they had roared away up the road like an Indian raid in the rosy twilight, and camped in back of the Moonview lot around a post with functioning speakers. The twins had brought blankets to sit on... which probably wasn't surprising.

The Moonview seemed immune to the mist, a mile up the road from the unlighted school, which looked like a haunted mansion at night, though Bilal had watched it drifting in beyond the zombie attacks on the screen. First it had snuffed out the bridge warning light, then it had slowly shrouded the town. Then it came creeping up the road to engulf the church and the Burger Barge and finally smother the school. Now it loomed like a ghostly wall maybe half a mile away.

The movie was almost over. Bilal knew the ironic ending, of course, but didn't want to be a spoiler. He was sitting with Chucky and Bucky, who were partially clad in 'beaters and jeans. Jody, also in 'beater, and back in his ragged old Levis, was sitting against the post. His narrow yellow eyes flew wide whenever a zombie chomped someone. Quentin, in his bully shirt, and Shawn in an old Gorillaz tee, were on the other side of the post, but not as close as they'd sat yesterday together in the boat.

They hadn't touched all evening, even naturally. At first it was only Quentin, who acted like Shawn had cooties, but they'd gone to the snack bar together -- though returning without any food -- and kept a distance ever since. Whatever they had talked about didn't seem to include Bilal... Shawn would have looked at him differently, maybe with anger or possibly fear. Now they looked like dudes in theaters who sat with an empty seat between them as if real men were afraid to touch after they'd gotten too old to be boys. Bilal had thought about clueing Quentin that acting too straight only looked gay, but maybe he'd done enough damage already to what should have been a beautiful thing.

Deputy Best's old Suburban rolled in past the ticket shack, dimming its lights to parking mode and trailing a tail of dust. There was a rain of beer bottles and cans being ejected from vehicles, and many red embers went out. There was a yell and a car stopped rocking. Bilal saw a figure in the back seat as the Suburban neared, and any street kid would have known it was cuffed.

The vehicle stopped nearby, and Deputy Best got out. "Evenin', guys. Got any beer?"

"We wish," said Chucky and Bucky together.

The deputy laughed. "Was hopin' I could bum one for the road." He paused to watch a zombie bite. "Sorry to bother you... looks like the best part, too... but could you all do me a favor?"

Everyone murmured assent.

"Just take a look at this boy," said Best. "An' let me know if you seen him before."

138

Everyone followed Best to the truck. He reached in and switched on the dome light, revealing a red-haired dude in back, skinny, and maybe seventeen. "This our drug-dealin' boy? ...You don't have to say, just give me a nod."

Everyone glanced at each other, then like a flash of ESP all the boys said, "yeah."

"Thanks," said Best. "Makes the paperwork easier, though we got him on possession already an' plenty to prove it's for sellin'. Would you stand by your word if it came to court?"

Quentin spoke first. "Yeah."

"Indubitably," said Jody.

"Seriously," said Shawn, who must have forgotten to play his new role and was standing close to Quentin.

"Zombie-easy," said Chucky and Bucky.

"Yeah," said Bilal. The dude in the car was looking at him. Naturally he was fronting bad, though Bilal could see the fear underneath. Maybe that was good? Like, maybe you needed a soul to be scared? To realize you'd done something wrong and know that some-thing, somewhere and some time, was going to punish you for it.

Best switched off the light. "Glad there's still a few men in this world. Gotta run this boy up to Stockton." Then he raised a hand. "By the power vested in me, you're all deputies till I get back."

Bilal smiled at the boy. "Later, alligator."

TWENTY-FOUR

The cracked chimes of Saint Toads clanked eleven times, muffled by the mist down the road as the last of the vehicles left though the gates like a rag-tag funeral procession. Dust settled slowly like sleepy ghosts sinking back into weedy graves in the dim yellow glow of a floodlight mounted above the tottering screen. Chucky finished rolling his blanket and lashed it to his ATV. "School tomorrow, dammit!"

Bucky mounted his machine. "Gotta learn the ways of the white-eyes to beat 'em at their game."

Chucky climbed onto his pony. "They stole our land, murdered most of our tribe, an' stuck the rest on a reservation, an' now that we're makin' some money they're taxin' us because *they're* broke!"

"We don't mean you guys," added Bucky, smiling at the other boys. "You're just white on the outside."

Jody laughed. "What about Bilal?"

"We're all the same on the inside," said Chucky.

Bilal wrapped the rope on the Gote's flywheel as Quentin got on the seat behind him. "That's gotta be gluttony, too," said Bilal. "Stealin' everything you can, then makin' people suffer to keep it."

Bucky nodded. "That's what the Creator said: the greedy ones will eat the world until there's almost nothin' left, but then they'll eat themselves."

"Maybe like *Soylent Green*," said Bilal.

Chucky added, "But then the earth will heal itself an' all the good people will live in peace like the Creator wanted us to."

"You mean the Great Spirit?" asked Bilal.

Bucky laughed. "Don't try an' talk red, you sound retarded."

"But, I thought you guys were Christians."

"There's only one Creator," said Chucky. "We trained our tongues to His Christian name, but He hears what's in our hearts."

Bucky added, "If we hadn't trained our tongues, there wouldn't be none of us left with hearts."

Bilal looked up at sky. "Do you believe there's a...?"

Chucky smiled. "Or duh."

Bucky added, "But don't say happy huntin' ground, that really sounds retarded."

Ringtones rang in stereo and the twins pulled out their phones. "Yeah, mom," said Chucky, "we're on our way."

"Yeah, dad," said Bucky, "we're on our way."

Jody climbed onto the back of Shawn's bike and clasped furry paws around Shawn's waist. Shawn kicked the starter and the engine snarled. A moment later the ATVs roared, their quad of headlights cutting the dust. Shawn switched on his light, which swept across the scabby screen as he revved the bike around the post, flinging up a spray of gravel. Bilal yanked the rope and the Gote's engine fired, belching blue smoke at a slow-thumping idle. He flipped a switch on the engine's magneto, but the bare light bulb in its tarnished reflector was about as bright as a birthday candle, the tail lamp only a cigarette glow. He looked out the gate at the wall of mist still looming a half mile away. "Hope I can find our way home."

"There's only one road," said Quentin. "Stay on it till you see the bridge light."

Bucky gunned his engine. "Follow your faithful Indian guides."

"Yeah," said Chucky. "Your friends to the end."

Quentin murmured in Bilal's ear, "God does not guide those who do evil but leaves them to wander in darkness."

Bilal replied, "But those who seek His light will see it."

The four machines rolled off to the gate through patches of gravel and dead yellow weeds, scattered beer bottles, cans and trash, awaken-ing sleepy ghosts again. Chucky and Bucky led the way, avoiding wet places and pizza-like puddles. Bilal followed them on the chugging Gote with Shawn tail-gunning behind. They reached the road and picked up speed, heading toward the wall of mist.

"Guess Annie is closed?" Bilal called to Quentin above the Gote's thumping beat.

Quentin, his arms around Bilal, pressed close to reply, "Only place for a burger now is Saunders Ferry an' that's ten miles."

"Damn," said Bilal.

"Got pizza in the freezer."

The Gote maxed-out at about thirty-five, and Chucky and Bucky were pulling ahead, but Shawn's light bobbing along behind was enough for Bilal to see. The Indian Summer night was warm, and the heat and throbbing pulse of the engine was morphing into his body. The air rushing past was scented with life, though he also sensed a sadness that he recognized as autumn, the old-age of a year. He'd felt it before in the city when pumpkins, even in the 'hood, began to grin on porches, but he'd never known what it was.

The twins burrowed into the misty wall like vanishing through a stargate. Bilal almost braced for impact, but only merged with nothingness. He felt a moment of fear as everything went ghostly gray, and cut the engine's throttle, but Quentin's grip around his waist tight-ened reassuringly. "Keep goin' or Shawn might hit us. Chucky an' Bucky slowed down, too... there's their lights."

Bilal saw a crimson glow ahead from Chucky and Bucky's tail lights. They had slowed to maybe twenty-five, and Bilal advanced his throttle to match. The beam of Shawn's light swept up behind, the sound of his engine muffled by mist. Bilal saw the road's faded center line flickering under his wheels and swung the Gote a bit to the right, then tracked the glow of the ATVs.

They must have been passing the school by now somewhere on the left, so The Burger Barge would be next on the right, though the lights of its sign were off. He swung a little more to the right, glimpsing weeds and spider webs beaded with jewels of mist. The shape of Annie's sign loomed up then disappeared behind. The church would be next, on his left, though he probably wouldn't see it. The twins could obviously see a lot better with their double-deuces of halogen and were slowly drawing away again. Bilal speeded up a little.

"Cool, huh?" said Quentin.

"Yeah, but kinda scary, too."

"That's part of what makes it cool."

The mist seemed a little colder tonight, its chill increased by the wind of the ride. Bilal wore Devon's white T-shirt, plastered now against his chest and reminding him that dudes had nipples, even if his were innies. Devon's jacket would have been nice, but no one else had brought a coat and Bilal hadn't wanted to look baby-ass. But the engine's heat was soaking his jeans, and its thrumming throb was matching his pulse. If he'd been alone on his own machine he might have let it happen in kid-like randiness.

He wondered if Devon was soaring above, like an expression, "the ghosts are flying." Or, had he finally gone to the light to ride a celestial minibike? Then he thought about Quentin and Shawn. Should he say anything about their new front? And their bully act might be hard to maintain since Chucky and Bucky had seen them naked in more ways than one yesterday. Jody might have sensed their love, but he'd been stoned all summer... though he seemed to be waking up now. But, who was Bilal to be preaching about how anybody should act?

The twins were drawing away again, probably eager for home and bed, and maybe a midnight raid on a fridge. Bilal speeded up a bit more. He wondered where Jadd Taimur had moved... to some other 'hood in some other city because he couldn't afford any better? Had he even been given a choice? He was old, black, and a Muslim in a country where some people hated all three and most had been taught to hate at least one.

Then he noticed a glow of headlights coming up the road from town. They seemed to be weaving side to side like somebody trying to stay on the road. Stop lights flared on the ATVs as Chucky and Bucky hit their brakes and swung to the right-hand shoulder. Bilal cut his throttle and pulled the Gote's brake, producing a squeal from the rear wheel band. He coasted into gravel and weeds, stopping about thirty feet from the twins, though all he could see was the glow of their lights and the oncoming beams of the car or truck, which seemed to be creeping at less than twenty. Shawn and Jody rolled up alongside.

"Some drunk?" asked Shawn.

Quentin studied the oncoming lights. "Looks more lost to me, but we better wait till it goes by." He pulled out his American Spirits, shook a cigarette up for Shawn, another for Jody, then one for himself and fired them with his lighter. "Happens sometimes," he said to Bilal after exhaling a ghost, "when it's real foggy like this. People take a wrong turn off the highway an' wander across the bridge into Rust."

"Then they're seriously lost," said Shawn. "'Cause nothin's open after nine so they can't get directions out of here."

"Probably what happened," said Quentin, as a vehicle half materialized like a partial transporter malfunction and stopped beside the twins. "Nobody 'round here drives a minivan, them things don't got no ground clearance."

Over the murmur of idling engines Bilal heard a mist-muffled voice. It seemed to be asking directions, though he couldn't make out the words. He turned toward the channel somewhere to the right. "We must be close to the hangin' tree."

Quentin pointed into the fog, though Bilal could see nothing but ghostly gray. "Over there, 'bout a hundred feet."

Gravel crunched under sneakers and Bucky's massive shape appeared in the dim yellow glow of the Gote's headlight. "Hey Bilal, your friends come to see ya."

TWENTY-FIVE

For a second Bilal sat frozen, the Gote's engine hot between his legs, exhaust pipe ghosting steam in the air, but his body turn-ing to ice. Then...

"Shit!" he hissed. "It's the Dubs!"

"Huh?" said Bucky.

Quentin didn't freeze. "Don't let your brother say nothin'!"

"You mean about Bilal?" asked Bucky. "Them guys were askin' where he lived."

Quentin scrambled off the bike. "Don't let Chucky tell 'em he's here! ...*Hurry*, man!"

Bucky broke into a ponderous run back to the ATVs, and Quentin spun around to Shawn. "Get out of here! Cut across the fields behind the church an' take the stage road back to town!"

But Shawn didn't move. "What's goin' on?"

An engine roared and tires burned. The minivan shot toward them!

"GO!" yelled Bilal. "They got guns!"

"Jody, hang on!" Shawn peeled a smoking one-eighty and blasted off into the mist.

There was a burst of full-auto fire and yellow-orange flame spat from the van! But Shawn's tail tight disappeared up the road, his engine snarl fading away.

"Quentin! DOWN!" Bilal dropped the Gote and tackled Quentin, both of them crashing into the weeds. Quentin flopped halfway into a ditch, and there was a slimy-sounding splash. The Gote toppled over a second later: its engine died and its lights went out. That must have been what saved them: the van shot past, still gaining speed.

Quentin struggled out of the ditch, his hair dripping muck, his shirt half soaked. He wiped his eyes and stared after the van, its tail lights vanishing in mist. "They must think it's you on the bike."

"Lucky for us." Bilal swiped a spider off his cheek, then rose to a crouch and peered up the road. "Will Shawn an' Jody be okay?"

Quentin stripped off his shirt and mopped mud from his face. "They're out in the fields by now, an' a minivan can't follow 'em there, even if they saw 'em turn off, an' they probably didn't."

Ponderous footsteps pounded the road as the twins came earth-quaking up, packing their feathered Yellow Boys.

"The fuck's goin' on?" panted Chucky.

"Yeah!" puffed Bucky. "The fuck's up with that?"

Quentin wiped slime off his chest. "Some boys from the 'hood are after Bilal."

"No shit?" asked Chucky.

"Or duh!" snapped Bucky. "Nobody 'round here's got a gun like that! They're only good for killin' people!"

"How many were there?" asked Bilal.

"Four like high school seniors," said Chucky.

"An' one about tenth grade," said Bucky.

"They're all black like you," added Chucky.

"They're black," said Bilal, "but not like me."

Quentin got to his feet, and Bilal pulled up his jeans. Quentin wiped more muck off himself, then tossed his shirt on the fallen Gote. "They're probably gonna be comin' back soon. They don't seem to know shit about drivin' in fog, but if they get up where it's clear they'll know they lost Shawn's bike." He turned to Chucky. "Did you tell 'em where Bilal's livin'?"

"Yeah. Sorry."

"You didn't know," said Bilal. Then he sighed. "The shitty thing about hiding shit is sometimes it gets you in deeper shit."

"What *is* this shit?" demanded Bucky.

"An' what are you hidin'?" asked Chucky.

"It's a gang," said Quentin. "They killed Bilal's friend an' he stood up in court, so three of 'em went to prison."

Bucky faced Bilal. "So now they wanna kill you?"

"It's stupid monkey games," said Bilal."

Chucky waddled out on the road and lay massively down with an ear to the pavement.

"That really work?" asked Bilal.

"Does for us," said Bucky.

"Somethin's comin'," said Chucky. "Still about a mile away. ...Too small for a truck an' not comin' fast. It's probably them."

Bucky considered. "Shawn woulda lost 'em at the church, an' they probably kept goin' as fast as they could, still thinkin' they could catch him. Then, when they busted out of the fog an' didn't see nothin' but empty road, they woulda turned around."

"Yeah," agreed Chucky. "Like Quentin said."

"He ain't as dumb as he looks," said Bucky.

Bilal stared into the mist up the road. "How the hell did they find me!"

Chucky got up and came over, sweeping his hair back over his shoulders. "That ain't important now, Bilal. What matters is that they did. They're goin' slow 'cause they're lost again, but they'll probably be here in about five minutes."

"Keep your ear to the ground," said Bucky.

Chucky returned to the road, and Bucky said, "Callin' 911 won't help. Deputy Best is gone, an' the closest cops are in Saunders Ferry."

"What kinda guns do they got?" asked Chucky, his ear to the pavement again.

"At least two AKs," said Bilal.

Bucky whistled. "If Custer had those he might have won."

"He could of brought Gatling guns," said Chucky. "But he was too full of himself."

"Lucky for us," said Bucky. "Shut up an' keep your ear to the ground."

"...There's somethin' else comin'! ...Fast!"

Bilal heard a bratty sound approaching up the road from town. Then the fog began to glow. A few seconds later Shawn rolled up. Jody was still behind him, and clutching Quentin's coach gun.

"Why'd you come back?" asked Quentin.

"To help my friends, duh!" Shawn saw Chucky's mass in the road. "Is he okay?"

Chucky smiled. "I'm just restin' so I won't get tired."

"Why'd you bring Jody?" asked Quentin. "Those fuckers are tryin' to *kill* people, man!"

"I kinda got that feelin' when the lead started flyin'." Shawn looked back at Jody. "He wanted to come. I thought about goin' home for my rifle, but that woulda taken too long, so we went to your house an' got that."

Jody gave the gun to Quentin. "An' here's da shells. ...An' I got dis, too." He pulled the Tokarev out of his jeans.

Bilal asked, "How'd you know I had that?"

"I just figured... 'cause you was black... so's I looked in your stuff."

"Thanks." Bilal took the gun. Then he saw blood on Jody's arm. "Did you get shot?"

"Ain't nuttin'," said Jody. "My aunt used ta hurt me way more den dat."

"I checked it," said Shawn. "Just nicked his shoulder like in a movie."

Chucky looked up from the road. "'Bout three minutes until they get here. Better figure out somethin', braves."

Bucky glanced at the ATVs, still idling though their lights were off. "Bilal, you an' Quentin ride home with us an leave the Gote here, we can go a lot faster."

"This is serious shit," said Bilal. "Monkeys kill people who help their victims."

"Yeah?" said Bucky. "If they come out on the reservation they'll never eat another banana."

Ringtones sounded. "You get it," said Chucky. "I'm busy."

Bucky pulled out his phone. "...Yeah, mom, we're cool... but... um... there's a problem. We'll have it fixed in a while. ...Yeah, I know." He made a face. "School tomorrow. Bye."

Quentin said, "That might be the best thing to do, Bilal. We can't go back to the house tonight 'cause they know where it is." He glanced up the mist-shrouded road. "An' they can't be stupid enough

148

to stay around till mornin' 'cause they'll figure we called the cops."

"Yeah," said Shawn. "If they got any brains, they'll find the bridge an' get their asses out of town."

Bilal felt suddenly alone despite everyone around him. He turned to Quentin. "It's not just tonight. They'll come back. They gotta kill me to prove they're monkeys to other monkeys. It could be tomorrow… or anytime. Maybe with you an' Shawn an' Jody." He turned to Bucky. "Or all of us together."

"Two minutes," called Chucky. "They're passin' Annie's."

Bilal looked down at the gun in his hand, then shoved it into his jeans. "I can call somebody."

"You mean go away?" asked Quentin.

"Maybe Mr. Skelly was right about black people bringin' problems."

"Hey!" said Bucky. "I thought we were friends."

"We are," said Bilal. "That's why I can't let you get in this shit."

"We're already in it," said Chucky. "We seen their faces, an' they shot at you… or somebody they thought was you."

"An' we ain't scared to say so," said Bucky.

"They shot at me," said Shawn. "An' I ain't scared to say so!"

"Dey did shoot me!" piped Jody. "An' I ain't scared ta say so neither! Unintimitably!"

Bilal only sighed. "That's what I mean about bringin' problems."

Chucky got up and waddled over. "I don't know how it works in the 'hood, but here we're *really* friends to the end."

Bucky smiled. "This is the part where we pull out the knife an' become blood brothers."

Chucky looked up the road where the mist was beginning to glow. "'Cept we ain't got time for the blood."

"Here's mine," said Jody offering his arm.

"Thanks," said Bilal. "All of you. But, what if that ain't enough to put the monkeys in a cage? I been though all that shit in court. The minivan's gotta be boosted, so even if we get the license that won't prove the monkeys were in it." He faced the twins. "Their lawyer will say it was dark an' foggy so how could you be *sure* it was them." He spread his hands. "I saw three of them kill my friend from ten feet away in the daytime. An' that almost wasn't enough."

"We'll talk about that later," said Bucky. "Quentin, stash the Gote in the weeds."

Chucky looked up the road again at the steadily brightening glow. "Or, we could stop the monkey shit here."

TWENTY-SIX

"**W**hat do you mean?" asked Bilal.

Bucky fingered his rifle, somehow no longer just a fat kid but something very dangerous. "They're only goin' about fifteen. We take both sides of the road. They'll never see us in the fog. We shoot out their tires first, zombie-easy."

"...You mean do a massacre?" asked Bilal.

Chucky said, "The worst punishment our tribe ever had was banishing someone who killed anybody."

Bucky nodded. "We believed that human beings should never take a human life."

Chucky shot a scowl up the road. "But they ain't human beings no more 'cause they lost their spirit light."

Quentin checked that his shotgun was loaded. "What do you wanna do, Bilal? Whatever it is, I'm in."

"So are we," said Chucky. He touched Jody's arm. "Can we borrow some of this?"

"Help yourself," said Jody.

Chucky swiped a finger in blood and made two stripes on his chubby cheeks, then Bucky did the same. A moment later so did Quentin. It should have been funny, but it wasn't.

Bilal looked back up the road, where the glow in the mist was defining itself into a pair of headlights. He gripped the gun in his jeans. What was he waiting for? A sign from Allah? A sanction from Devon?

"Shawn," said Quentin, "you an' Jody get out of here."

Shawn scowled. "'Cause we don't have guns?"

"So you don't have to get in this shit."

JESS MOWRY

"I'm stayin'!" snarled Jody. "I can throw rocks!" He painted two stripes on his fuzzy cheeks.

"Me too!" said Shawn, also blooding himself.

Bilal's own voice surprised him. "No! We can't!"

Quentin asked, "This the part where you're gonna say 'cause then we ain't no better than them?"

"I could quote the Quran about mercy."

"Or about killin' your enemies."

"I could do the same with the Bible, but I only know what I feel." Bilal faced the twins and patted his chest. "I hear my heart." Then he asked, "What happened to somebody when they got banished?"

"They could live if they wanted to," said Bucky. "Wander the earth all alone."

"An' ask the Creator for mercy," said Chucky.

"Like goin' to prison," said Bilal. "Except they were locked outside, not in." He glanced at the oncoming lights. "Sometimes you can find what you lost."

"What you mean?" asked Shawn. "Like, try an' take 'em prisoner? Like we was really deputies? Hey, they got *machine guns*, man! If we don't kill 'em, they'll kill us!"

Bilal tried to think. "We could shoot out their tires like Bucky said. Where they gonna go on foot?"

"Follow the road back to town," said Chucky, "an' steal another car."

Bucky nodded. "Or maybe jack one an' shoot somebody."

"We could shoot 'em in da legs," said Jody.

Quentin shook his head. "Then it would be like we attacked them. It's like Bilal said about lawyers an' courts... *they* would look like victims. If we have to shoot 'em, we have to kill 'em, or it might be us in a cage."

Shawn faced the oncoming lights. "We better figure out somethin'!"

Quentin gave the shotgun to Jody. "Shawn! You an' Jody go back to my house."

"But..."

"GO!"

152

"Hang on, Jody!" Shawn revved his bike, burned a one-eighty, and bratted away in the mist.

"Bilal," said Quentin. "Start the Gote. Bucky, give Bilal your phone."

"Got a plan?" asked Bucky, tossing his phone to Bilal.

"I hope so... it's all I can think of." Quentin helped Bilal pick up the Gote. "We ride to my house as fast as we can."

"Then get on with us," said Chucky.

"I'm goin' with you, but Bilal stays here." Quentin faced Bilal. "You trust me?"

"Yeah," said Bilal.

"Then do exactly what I say."

"I don't get it," said Bucky.

"Me neither," said Chucky. "They wanna kill him an' you're leavin' him here?"

"Mount up, I be with you in a minute."

The twins looked puzzled but lumbered off to their ATVs. Quentin waited as Bilal wrapped the rope and spun the Gote's engine to life. The lights came on dimly but Quentin killed them. "Ride across the ditch an' turn around. Just far enough so the monkeys won't see you. Don't go no further, you might lose the road or run into the channel. Wait till I call you, then do what I say. ...*No matter what.* Okay?"

"Understood."

"Lose your shirt, it's white, you're not."

Bilal shed his shirt, then asked, "Got any blood left?"

Quentin touched a finger to his cheek, then striped blood on Bilal's. "Go, man."

Bilal gunned the Gote through the mucky ditch as Quentin ran to the ATVs. A moment later they roared away, leaving Bilal alone in the mist now glowing pale from the oncoming lights. He turned the bike around and stopped. Over the engine's chugging idle he heard the approaching van. The monkeys were obviously lost again: he pictured their heads out the windows as they tried to stay on the road. He gripped the pistol in his jeans. It would be easy to kill them now; hide in the ditch, take out a tire, and stay camouflaged in the dark. Five of them, and he had eight shots. Take his time and aim at their heads. Zombie-easy; a kid could do it.

But, that was part of the problem.

The van crept past at maybe fifteen. Bilal heard voices... "the fuck's that motherfuckin' bridge!" The tail lights left a bloody glow that slowly faded away. Then Bilal was in nothingness and couldn't see the road anymore. He looked over his shoulder: there seemed to be a darker darkness looming at his back... probably the hanging tree. "Devon?" he whispered, releasing the gun and grasping the charm. "I'm scared, man."

The church bell started its countdown to midnight. Over the lonely-sounding clanks Bilal heard a distant rumbling; maybe a truck rolling through town. Then, ringtones startled him. He squinted at the phone's little screen and figured out which button to push. "Yeah?"

Quentin's voice: "They pass you yet?"

"Yeah, just now."

"Ride for the bridge as fast as you can. Get ahead of 'em. You'll see the green light. Go for it no matter what happens! Straight for the light an' don't slow down!"

"...You mean cross the bridge?"

"Straight for the light. ...*No matter what*!"

"Understood," said Bilal, though he didn't. What good would it do to cross the bridge? If they were going to ambush the Dubs, they should have done it here. But he shoved the phone in a pocket and found the light switch on the engine's magneto. The bare bulb came on dimly, no brighter than a jack 'o lantern. He still couldn't see the road, but the Gote was facing that way so he throttled up and rolled through the weeds. There was the ditch. He gunned the bike through and onto the pavement, then twisted the throttle wide open. Without Quentin's weight the Gote went faster, maybe up to forty. The mist was cold on his shirtless body, but he concentrated on the dim white line flickering past on his left.

Then he saw a faint red glow ahead... the bridge warning light? No, he hadn't gone that far. He was catching up with the monkeys. Quen-tin had said to pass them... and keep going no matter what.

But, how could he get around them? For a second he almost slowed down. Then he pulled the gun from his jeans, clamped its barrel between his teeth, flattened himself to the bike's gas tank, head thrust over the handle-bars, and kept the throttle wide open.

The van was only creeping, tracking the road's centerline. Which side should he try to pass? The driver's side... one less gun. He swung to the left, his body pressed tight to the throbbing machine. He was almost past the driver's window. He caught a glimpse of a monkey face. For an instant there was no recognition. Then...

"THAT'S HIM!"

Then he was past. Over his pounding engine beat he heard the van speed up. The full-auto rip was no surprise, bullets hissing over his head. Another rip. Should he shoot back? That might make them careful. He aimed his gun blindly over a shoulder and pulled the trigger twice. The kick was more then he expected. The blast made his ear go numb. The bullets could have gone anywhere, but the monkeys must have seen the flashes because the van dropped back a little.

Then he saw a faint green glow... the traffic light on the bridge. The throttle was already maxed but he twisted it even harder as if that could somehow force more speed, and shoved the gun back in his jeans. Another rip of auto-fire! Bullets hissing past his ear. He found the switch and killed the lights, aiming for the emerald blur. The van was gaining fast!

Then he felt arms around his chest, and a heavy soft warmth on his back. ...*How could a ghost be warm?* A voice in his ear...

"It's your friend to the end," said Devon.

Bilal kept his eyes on the misty green glow, the engine pounding under him. "Is this the end?"

"If I could tell your future you wouldn't be in this shit. ...This might be a good time to pray."

"I prayed for you an' He didn't do nothin'!"

"Yeah He did, He saved you."

Another rip of auto-fire, and ricochets twanged from the bridge iron ahead just like movie FX. The van was catching up! The green glow was defining itself into the traffic light over the road. ...But something was wrong!

"Don't lose your light," said Devon.

Bilal almost cut the throttle. Almost yanked the brake. But then it was too late. The light was green on the tower. The wooden arm stood vertical.

But there was *nothing* ahead!

Devon laughed. "Good thing you learned how to swim."

Then Bilal was flying in darkness, the Gote's engine roaring, its wheels clawing mist. Behind he heard the scream of tires.

"I'd get off here," said Devon.

Bilal leaped away from the falling bike. The tumble though space seemed to go on forever. There were crazily jumbled images... the iron skeleton high above, the cart-wheeling Gote smacking the water, headlights stabbing the mist overhead... and the underside of a minivan.

Then he plunged into liquid blackness. For a second he almost panicked, but this was like dropping off the rope into McElligot's Pool.

The water was maybe ten feet deep -- *dredging the channel ain't 'green'* -- and he hit the bottom in movie slow motion. He kicked up from the mud and surfaced. The first thing he heard were screams of terror. The cries were almost comical... *Help! Help! I can't swim!*

Then, warning bells began to clang. The traffic lights went red, and the wooden arms came creaking down. Bilal treaded water and turned toward the cries. The van's tail lights were still on, its ass-end still above the surface like a diving duck. Maybe it was floating, or maybe its nose was jammed in the mud. There were burbling sounds like the car in *Psycho*. Four of the monkeys now clung to the van after fighting each other to get out the windows. The fifth, the youngest, was floun-dering maybe ten feet away, but none the others were going to help.

The four older monkeys had spotted Bilal. They cursed him with all the baby-talk words any third-grader knew, almost drowning the younger boy's cries. Bilal heard an outboard motor start up. But the younger boy was going down.

My anger is tempered by mercy.

Bilal swam to the boy and snagged his hood, pulling his head back above the surface. The boy thrashed and spluttered. "Help me!"

"Chill out!" yelled Bilal. "Or I'll let go!" He yanked the pistol from his jeans and aimed at the terrified face, but the boy was too scared of the water to be afraid of a gun.

Then Shawn's voice: "Don't let him grab you! He'll pull you both down!"

Bilal shoved the gun back in his jeans and stayed behind the struggling boy, keeping a one-handed grip on his hood while kicking to keep them both afloat. Out of the mist came the shabby orange boat riding low in the water. Shawn was running the motor, and the twins were standing with their rifles. Jody was in the bow, the shotgun in his paws, and all the steel was aimed at the monkeys.

Shawn eased the boat up to the struggling boy, who grabbed the bow in a death grip. "Just hold on!" warned Jody steadily aiming the gun. "You try an' climb in an' I cap your dumb ass! Unremorsefully!"

"Same goes for you!" Shawn called to the others. "Stay on the van!"

"What if it sinks?" cried one.

"Can't *none* of you swim?" asked Bucky.

The monkeys just looked stupid, as if he'd asked if they could fly. Chucky shrugged. "Guess it ain't required in monkey-boy land."

"You okay, Bilal?" asked Shawn.

"Yeah."

Jody laughed. "You shoulda seen yourself flyin'!"

Shawn guided the boat to the mired van, and Bucky gestured with his rifle to the clinging boy. "Get over there with your friends!"

"Yeah!" added Jody, "da friends ta *your* end!"

There was a sticker on the van's rear window:

MOM'S TAXI

Shawn backed the boat away after the boy had grabbed the van's bumper... none of the others helping him. "Bilal. Can you swim to the dock? We're a little overloaded."

"We'll watch the monkeys," said Chucky.

"Sorry, don't got no bananas," Jody called to the stranded boys.

Bucky said, "Don't look like the van's gonna sink any more, an' Deputy Best should be comin' back soon."

Quentin's voice called from up on the tower. "Okay to close it?"

"Yeah!" called Shawn.

Bilal dog-paddled for the dock as the bridge began to rumble and clank. He felt the pistol under his belly, colder than the water.

"You sure now?" asked Devon's voice.

Bilal looked up: Devon sat on the base of the tower smiling like he always did. "What should I do?"

"Life don't come with instructions," said Devon. "Sometimes you just gotta do what you feel."

"Like, in your heart? Or in your soul?"

"Don't matter what you call it," said Devon. "But if you got one you'll know what's right."

Bilal pulled the gun from his jeans and let it fall into the darkness.

Devon pointed a chubby finger. "By the way, it's up there."

"The light?" asked Bilal.

"Got stuck in a pulley, or whatever it's called. Been goin' round an' round for years. Figured Quentin would wanna know."

"...Oh," said Bilal.

The bridge closed with a massive CLUNK. The warning bells stopped, the lights went green, and the wooden arms lifted to point at the sky. Still smiling, Devon faded away. "Later, alligator."

TWENTY-SEVEN

everend Bray didn't hesitate before speaking the name of God -- one of His infinite number of names -- as he finished reading the service. "Praise be to Allah the Merciful, and guide us on the right path."

"On whose name be praise," said Bilal.

The reverend returned the Quran to Quentin, then drew a Bible from his pocket. "Would you mind...?"

Quentin smiled. "No problem." He looked down at the freshly-filled grave. There was a shiny new headstone carved with the name, Taimur, and a crescent moon. "I know he won't mind."

"I've also done Buddhist services, as well as Native-American." Reverend Bray opened his Bible and read another funeral verse.

"Dat's almost da same," whispered Jody.

"Good stuff always is," said Bilal.

"Seriously," murmured Shawn.

Chucky and Bucky smiled.

The people seemed to notice that, too, some looking surprised while others just nodded. Most of the town was there, including the Indian families. Mr. Skelly, clad in black, looked like either an under-taker or something that should have been taken under. Mrs. Wicket was dabbing her eyes; Annie and Deputy Best had their hats off; and Mr. Gilman stood beside them. Only Jody's aunt looked pissed, like something sinful was going down but Jesus wouldn't give her a spirit.

Darien, Quentin's older brother, stood on the other side of the grave. It was no surprise he was huge, a grown-up Kung Fu Panda.

Jadd Taimur, in kufi and robe, stood nearby with Mark and

Akeem, who were clad in regular clothes. He'd gotten many curious looks, but word had apparently gotten around -- probably from Deputy Best -- that he'd bought a house on the channel. One with a dock for a boat. This was his second time in Rust: Akeem had driven him here last week to look at the house Bilal had found. The price had been divinely low.

Reverend Bray closed his Bible, and the people began to leave. Mr. Gilman was talking to Deputy Best: "...As long as they don't shop at Walmart!"

Darien gave Quentin a panda bear hug. "I got a presentation to-morrow, but I'll be back on Tuesday. You did the right thing, little bro."

Quentin smiled at Bilal. "Nah, he did."

Mrs. Marsh, the post office lady, came up to Quentin as Darien left. "I keep forgetting," she said, "you owe me for a stamp."

"Huh?" said Quentin.

"I mailed your letter last week. You must have dropped it in Gilman's. He brought it over to me."

"Oh," said Quentin, and dug in his jeans for change. "Thanks."

"Sorry, Bilal," said Jody. "I went ta get a candy bar an' it musta falled outta my pocket. Dat musta been how dem monkeys found ya."

"Yeah," said Bilal. "They wouldn't tell the cops nothin'. It's part of the stupid monkey game. But they'll be in cages awhile... which is also part of the game."

"Inevitably," said Jody.

Bilal looked up at the sky. The air was a little cooler today -- the old-age of another year -- but the channel glistened under the sun, and the land and hills were gold in the light. Then he smiled at Jody. "Maybe you saved a soul or two."

Quentin added, "Or maybe gave somebody time to figure out they had one."

"...Oh," said Bilal to Jody. "I got somethin' for you. My grand-father brought it from Sudan; it's an African flute."

"Goody! Tanks!"

"Zombie cool hat, Bilal," said Shawn.

Bilal touched his leather kufi and smiled. "Who says Muslims can't be cool?"

"Could I get one, or is that forbidden?"

"Bein' cool is never forbidden."

"Are you gonna start prayin'?" asked Quentin.

Bilal looked around the graveyard, where crosses surrounded him. "Maybe I never really stopped. Like, inside where it counts."

Chucky nodded. "Words don't mean nothin' if your heart ain't talkin'."

"Or your light ain't shinin'," said Bucky.

Jadd Taimur raised a palm to Bilal in the universal sign of peace. "I will see you at home."

"May Allah be with you," said Bilal.

"On whose name be praise. And with you, grandson."

Bilal watched his grandfather, Mark and Akeem roll off in Akeem's Explorer. Then he turned to Quentin. "Sometimes you do things to make people happy, an' that makes God happy, too."

Jody grinned. "An' you'd get outta class for a while everday."

All the people had left by now in dusty cars and pickups, the Indian families in flatbed trucks, heading for the rusty bridge whose towers loomed above the willows. The bell of Saint Toads began clanking noon. Chucky and Bucky stripped off their shirts like savages going back to the wild, and everyone else did the same. Then the boys walked through waist-high weeds to where the ATVs were parked. There was also a pair of battered Tote Gotes... Quentin had built a second machine from dissected corpses and extra parts after they'd rescued his from the channel.

Bilal wrapped a rope on his Gote's flywheel, and Jody climbed onto the seat at his back as Chucky and Bucky mounted their ponies. Quentin boarded his machine and Shawn squeezed on behind, putting his arms around Quentin.

"Um?" asked Bilal, before starting his engine. "What are you guys gonna do?"

"You mean about lettin' our light shine?" asked Shawn.

"Well," said Quentin, "you're wearin' a kufi." He turned to Shawn. "Sometimes you gotta do what you feel."

Jody laughed. "So, kiss him why don't ya."

Quentin did, and everyone else made awwwww sounds.

"I know what I feel," said Bucky. "Like Tugboat Triples at Annie's."

"Yeah," said Chucky. "With blueberry sundaes."

Jody piped few notes on his flute as if he'd been playing it all his life. "Den let's go swimmin', brothers!"

END

ABOUT THE AUTHOR

Jess Mowry was born in 1960 near Starkville, Mississippi. When he was only a few months old his father took him to live in Oakland, California. Mowry's father was a voracious reader who introduced his son to books at a very early age. Jess attended a public school, but despite his love of reading, dropped out at age thirteen, part way through the eighth grade and worked with his father in the scrap-iron business. In his late teens, Jess moved to Arizona to work as a truck driver and heavy equipment operator. He also lived and worked in Alaska as an engineer aboard a tugboat and as an aircraft mechanic on Douglas C-47 cargo planes, as well as at a children's refuge in Haiti.

Mowry has written twenty-five books and many short stories about black children and teens in a variety of genres, ranging from inner-city settings to the forests of Haiti, the wilds of Alaska, the Arizona desert, the Caribbean Sea, and the African veldt. While some of his novels are set in Oakland and deal with social issues, such as poverty, violence, drugs, gangs, teenage sexuality, and school drop-outs, Mowry has also written ghost tales, as well as novels featuring Voodoo and African magic, in addition to sea stories, and compiled an anthology of Victorian ghost stories.

Jess Mowry lives in Oakland, California.

THIS BOOK IS ALSO AVAILABLE IN A KINDLE EDITION

OTHER ANUBIS BOOKS

AVAILABLE ON AMAZON